THE
LENIN PIN

RALPH SCHNEIDEMAN

Trea KL Publishing LLC
Seattle

Publisher's Note
This is a work of semi-fiction. Names, characters, places and incidents have been changed fictitiously to protect the innocent or are the product of the author's imagination and any resemblance to actual persons, living or dead, organizations or technologies, events or associated locales is outrageously coincidental.

Trea KL Publishing LLC.
4739 44th Avenue S.W. No.403
Seattle, WA. USA 98109
info@treaKLpublishing.com

First American edition
10 9 8 7 6 5 4 3 2 1

LIBRARY OF CONGRESS CATALOGING IN PUBLICATION DATA
The Lenin Pin / Ralph Schneideman
ISBN 978-0-578-10400-3
Fiction-Espionage--Moscow--Paris--Genève.
Schneideman, Ralph
Title

Registered. Writers Guild of America, West, Inc
1531264 09/07/11

Graphics by NZ Graphics, Denver

For TC, who unribbons my heart.

TO THE READER
Kia Ora, and thank you for purchasing a copy of my manuscript, 'The Lenin Pin.' I hope that you will recommend it to friends and others. I am excited to see what a creative, viral network can lead to!

PROLOGUE

THE FINANCIAL TIMES, Wednesday, March 24, 2011

By Robin Harding in Tokyo

"Toshiba is talking to a company backed by Microsoft Chairman Bill Gates about a joint development of a nuclear reactor with the potential to run for 100 years without refuelling.

Toshiba emphasized that the discussions were preliminary and have so far involved only an exchange of information."

CHAPTER I

Moscow.

At first the fire was not visible. Guilt-by-proximity was enough not to linger in the vicinity of Lubiana and the tired façade of the building that contained the fire was located only one block away from the prison. People worked here, they passed through the neighborhood, but they did not live here. It was a Sunday and the street was almost empty. Those who traversed the cobblestones kept their heads down against the chill of the skirting wind that carried snow that harassed them.

It was not until the sound of shattered glass fragments sparkled down through the wire mesh fronting every window from the fifth through seventh floors that any protest was heard.

A Policeman later recalled that chards fell from 'every window almost at the same time.' But it was only the billowing smoke that identified the fire and only the sound of sequenced fire alarms that identified its locations.

The drive-through front doors of the building remained closed to the inner courtyard, barring any thought of entry by those on the street to raise further alarm.

The tradesman door remained closed, inferring emptiness behind its worn appearance until a figure, in military uniform, stepped through and onto the pavement.

The sound of sirens drew the few who witnessed the event to congregate opposite the doors that were opened outward to allow ingress to the fire engine that slowed as it approached the military officer who directed it inward. No-one observed or at least did not comment on the fact that the engines were military green and not the Moscow Municipal Fire Department red and gold.

CHAPTER ll

New York

"Mr. Judd, I'm Anthony Booth. Welcome to Gulf Resources."

Judd studied the hands and the face across the table as the man offered his Business Card. Starched shirt, the right amount of cuff exposing the watch, designer tie, banker's glasses. First impression: too damned tight.

"I'll get right to the point, Mr. Judd. Your oil experience will serve you well for the consulting position that we're offering you. You are recently divorced and,' the man looked up feigning surprise, 'and did not contest the proceedings which means that you're free to travel as required! You have no stock in our Company, and never have had which is another positive in your favor." Booth hesitated, frowning, rereading his notes in exaggerated surprise. "In fact, you've never owned any stock, and you don't own your car either, a 2004 BMW with one year left on a lease!"

"Are you married, Mr. Booth?" Ethan interrupted quietly, impatient, turning the focus. Booth sat back in his chair, surprised by the interruption.

"Children?" Ethan continued.

Booth responded in the negative. He queried Ethan's smile. "Is there something I've missed?'

"No, it's just that if your file is as complete as you say it is, you will know that I have one daughter in her second year at Oxford and another in ballet and I'm surprised that you wonder why I don't own any stock!!"

It was the first consulting prospect he'd had since his self-imposed sabbatical, following his divorce. Six months exploring Tuscany, a journey he had always expected to take with Christine. Twenty years had passed and it never happened. There were the girls and his work, and, and now, he needed the income; he needed the alimony payment and the child support. But not from a self-centered middle manager like this. He waited for Booth.

"This is a temporary assignment, Mr. Judd. You speak Russian and that will hold you in good stead," Booth cleared his throat, at a loss for words other than those that he read, "You were your Company's liaise with your Russian oil counterpart in Iraq before the first Gulf War and your passport is still valid. I'm authorized to offer you three thousand dollars a day plus expenses. The assignment should last for six working days, but we'll pay you for ten."

Ethan put his fingertips together and raised them to his lips. Tight, too damned tight. Reaching forward he retrieved the business card from the polished desktop and studied it in silence.

"Your card reads, 'Vice President,' Mr. Booth. Why do you have the responsibility for this hire?"

Booth's cheeks reddened. "The program is my responsibility!"

"Are you sure that your boss isn't just distancing himself or herself from you in case something goes wrong?"

Booth covered quickly, but not quick enough to cover a momentary glimmer of doubt, of insecurity in his eyes. "Absolutely not! This program is mine; I've been involved in all of the critical developments for over one year now."

"But are you a decision maker or are you just a messenger?"

"I can assure you."

"No, you can't Mr. Booth but for the moment we'll leave the issue open. What is the assignment?"

Booth dropped the volume of his voice as he leaned forward in a conspiratorial gesture, pushing a manila envelope across the table. "We will of-course request a Non-Disclosure Agreement from you, and if you'll deliver your passport to my office this afternoon, we'll have it couriered to Washington for your visa and returned by tomorrow morning."

Ethan nodded, a tacit recognition that the normal channels of the Russian Consulate were being circumvented.

"We've arranged for you to attend an oil equipment tradeshow in Moscow, beginning four days from now, as a member of the delegation of one of our subsidiary companies. Your assignment, however, is to privately deliver for signature a set of protocol papers to a ranking member of the Iranian Parliament who will also attend the show. His photograph is in the envelope. You're to deliver those papers back to our Paris office. If the documents aren't signed or aren't returned to you within three days you're to continue on to Paris and consider your assignment fulfilled. We expect that."

"And the US Embargo!"

'Does not affect us. We're not doing business in Iran. We're not exporting there and we're not buying anything from them. We're quite within the letter of the law."

"Excuse me," Ethan interrupted again, opening the envelope, studying the photograph. "My concern is not the Company at this point in time. Where is the risk? What's in these protocol papers as you call them that your Company does not want to be identified with, that you're willing to pay me thirty thousand dollars to deliver?"

Caught in the excitement of his ego, Booth continued without realizing his misunderstanding of the direction of the question. "Putin's' still having his problems and we can't afford to back a losing horse as though to speak. So, we're spreading our risk! We've negotiated, on behalf of a consortium group, including the Iranians, oil exploration rights within the Republic of Kazakhstan. We've committed to revitalize certain of Kazakhstan's oil and gas fields, and," he drew the word out for emphasis, "and, we will help them with gas pipeline distribution into Western Europe."

Ethan struggled not to show his surprise as he digested the enormity of the transaction. He pushed the photograph back across the table.

"Mr. Booth, you misunderstand my question. Where is the risk for me?"

"There is none," Booth smiled, his arms outstretched, "as long as you don't let the documents fall into the hands of the Russian executive authorities. Putin's people would not be too happy if they found that we have been negotiating with his opposition and playing both ends against the middle!" Exaggerating his gesturing in dismissal, he continued, "They may never grant you another visa, but, at worst, they'll deport you as an undesirable. In the long run, they need us. Nothing else will happen. It's really a trust issue!"

"Then why risk it?" Ethan queried, his curiosity piqued by the potential of the deal.

"No risk, Mr. Judd, as long as you don't screw up!"

The smugness of the words irritated Ethan. Producing a pack of cigarettes and matches he sat backwards in his chair, creating a silence across the mahogany desk. He smiled at the Booth through a tumble of smoke as he lit a cigarette and placed the spent match back in its box.

"Why have you waited until four days before the show to organize this side venture? He asked quizzically. "Why don't you or some up-and-coming junior executive act as messenger for the company? I would have thought that dealing with the Iranians who seem to be persons non gratis with anyone in the world today would be risky business?"

Booth shook his head as if having to patiently explain a history lesson before he answered. "If you're referring to Ahmedinejad, Mr. Judd, his stance is just rhetoric. He is tolerated by both sides. Our relationship with the National Iranian Oil Company goes back to the mid 30's, before the time of the Shah. It's not going to change. They need US dollars and we need the oil. The American people may not like it if they knew that most of us are still dealing with the Iranians but they're really not interested in the details. In the end it's all about more gas in the tank for Californians and heating oil in the Northeast in winter, not conservation or moral imperatives." Lecture over, Booth continued: "I'll be coordinating everything from Paris. Outside of that, as I told you, this is a one shot transaction and we just don't want any negative exposure for the Company."

The man's time dilemma was not lost to Ethan.

"Please thank the company for the offer, Mr. Booth. I will consider it and get back to you tomorrow."

"No," the man's anxiety jumped at him, "I must have your commitment now, before you leave my office! We know you're not working. I don't understand your hesitation! Three thousand a day is a lot of money. Why do you need until tomorrow?"

Ethan inhaled on his cigarette and exhaled before he responded,

"Maybe you're right!" He nodded as if in resignation of his predicament. "I will agree to five thousand dollars a day for this assignment, plus expenses, and I will call my own schedule. I want fifty percent of my fees in advance with a minimum contract of one month!" He smiled to conclude the bluff. He could use the work, but if they said no, he would re-negotiate with an insincere comment about the hope for future work with the Company etc that neither side would be interested in. There was no need.

Booth squinted fiercely, as if drawn by the brightening glow of the cigarette as Ethan inhaled again, deliberately.

"Okay, five thousand a day. You'll report directly to me and ten days from today you must be in Paris with the document package. You'll hand it directly to me, no one else."

"In your office?"

"No," Booth snapped, feeling himself back in control. "If you insist on your own schedule, make your own reservations and let me know whatever hotel you'll be staying at. You'll deliver the documents to me there." "This is important to the Company, Judd," he continued aggressively, "it's not a difficult assignment, don't screw it up! You're getting paid a lot of..."

Ethan raised the palm of his hand, cutting Booth off in mid-sentence.

"It's important to your future, Tony, is it?" he asked, frowning, using the man's first name, exaggerating the intimacy between them.

Booth searched Ethan's eyes for an equal clarity of understanding, a recognition of trust. He spoke, disarmed.

"Yes, it is, in all honesty," he added, almost in protest.

"Then Tony, if you don't screw it up, we'll be okay." Ethan cut to the man's insecurity. "I don't have any interest in a long-term relationship with this Company or with you personally, so you don't have to consider me a threat. "Give me what I need and I'll deliver. But remember," he continued with a conciliatory smile, "I'm your meal ticket. Short change me, and you short change yourself!"

Booth pursed his lips, the frown lines around his eyes betraying some inner frustration.

"Okay," he nodded, "I understand. If there has been any misunderstanding, I . . .'Ethan rose from his chair and moved towards the door of the office.

"I want the details of the assignment and a cashier's check delivered to my apartment this afternoon when you pick up my passport. And please include a twenty thousand dollar expense advance in the check and," he smiled, "I'll see you in Paris in ten days."

Booth did not stand as his consultant departed from his office.

CHAPTER lll

Moscow

Andre Cosarkov sat as comfortably as he could at parade rest in
the anti-chamber, awaiting the beckoning of the electric buzzer that would
prompt him to move into the next room. He was self-conscious. A solitary
figure, isolated in a room designed and decorated to accommodate the ease
and full complement of Russia's Czarist military command elite one
hundred years before his time. He had never before been ordered to the
General's office. His nervousness was mixed with speculations at being
called to this inner-sanctum.

He tried to relax. Vertebrae popped as he stretched his shoulder
backward. He gazed idly at the irregular pattern in the red mahogany
paneled wall that confronted him and then at the military paintings, battle
scenes and uniforms and medals, accentuated in cracked white acrylics that
linked him to their presence over the paneling. Heroic faces in alert
attendance, their eyes fixed outwardly somewhere over his head, beyond
the confines of the room towards moments and memorials long since
neglected; their group consciousness long since lost to a thinning
generation of silent patriots. He studied the right leaning brush strokes until
the muffled ring of the buzzer commanded his attention. He moved across
the hardwood floor toward the beckoning command of the closed doors.
Pulling his shirt sleeves down he was conscious that the impact of his heel
plates accentuated the shortened gait of his left leg; conscious that he was

about to enter into the Office of the Director of Internal Military State Security for what reason he did not know.

The door opened inward as if on command as he lifted his right hand to knock. He took in the colonel's epaulets of the man who held the door for him to enter as he recovered with a formal nod of courtesy. He recognized the battle decorations, the qualifications, the statement of the man's contribution to his place in his world.

Eight steps marched him to the center of the room. Snapping to attention he saluting over the flat crown of white hair that confronted him, his sight riveted through the ornate French window panes that framed his General.

"Major Andre Illyach Cosarkov reporting as ordered, General, Sir." He waited.

The old man began slowly, looking up, the depth of timbre in his voice vibrating the air between them. "Andre Cosarkov," He dismissed his aide with a gesture of a hand held away from his body, dissipating the smoke from a smoldering cigarette. He labored for another breath. "I knew your father. We were in Czechoslovakia, in Prague together, in '56. Did he ever speak to you of me?"

"Yes, Sir. He had many stories of your exploits." He sensed the old man's smile.

"Cosarkov, you will address me as 'General,' which is my rank; or as 'General Itskov,' which is my rank and my name. No more 'Sir.'

"Yes, S . . . , Yes, General."

"And did your father tell you that he was my best tank commander?"

"No, General."

"Well, he was, but it is because your father was my trusted friend, that is why I have called you here today. It was your father's sacrifices for the Rodina that allowed you entry into the Academy. I have followed your progress since then." The statement was made matter-of-factly as the man drew heavily on his cigarette.

"It saddened me when he died. We were true comrades. But if you are anything like him your future will continue to be bright."

He moved the cigarette pack forward, offering it in a gesture of informality.

"Do you smoke? Sit, sit."

"Thank you, General." Cosarkov could feel the perspiration trickling down his armpits as he moved to the chair and sat.

The old man studied the campaign medals as they moved in parallel to the younger man's body, caught in the sun, reflecting off the cellophane of the American cigarette pack as he reached forward for it. To review and recognize the medals was to reinforce the task he was about to commit them both to.

"Andre Illyach Cosarkov, I am going to take you into my confidence. I have an assignment for which the utmost secrecy is required. It must never, and will never, be divulged, but those that matter know of it as they know that you are here today."

Cosarkov drew on his cigarette, filling the silence before the old man continued methodically, with studied command of the facts.

"Three days ago there was a fire in the Physics Department at the University of Moscow. Specifically, the fire occurred within the Applied Nuclear Physics laboratory. We have been supporting the development of a highly classified program within the laboratory and we do not believe that the fire was an accident."

"I do not remember reading of the fire, General."

"No, you did not, and you will not."

The old man paused, lighting another cigarette from the first not yet extinguished. His eyes were bright, riveted on the son of his friend seated, bathed in smoky light before him.

"We believe that the fire was set deliberately, set to cover the theft of critical working papers related to our project."

"And may I know the nature of that project, General?"

He watched the man smile. False teeth, the only unnaturalness of his seventy-five plus years.

"A rather remarkable nuclear technology, Cosarkov. Its origin is actually American. A clipping service found a preliminary technical paper published in an investment journal and forwarded it to us. It seems that the author of the paper was attempting to raise money to complete his research and to commercialize the technology."

"Excuse me, General, a clipping service?"

"An inexpensive and," Itskov smiled, "an absolutely legitimate American market research service. We would classify it as a specialized service of the old KGB. In America, it is a commercial opportunity. We give them a subject and, on an ongoing basis, they forward whatever their computers and readers find published."

"And the American efforts?"

"Let us just say that despite their best efforts, they were not successful in completing their proof of technical feasibility studies, nor in raising their investment to continuing the work. It was the genius of one man. Creative, but highly unstable. He was confined to a psychiatric hospital the last I heard. His ideas were discredited. It was at the height of the Cold War, you understand! He is now a ward of the state of New Hampshire."

Cosarkov watched the older man ease backward into his chair, the cigarette pluming from the distance of his outstretched arms. He did not ask for details of the technology transfer from New Hampshire to Moscow University, he could read between the lines. He nodded in acknowledgment of the explanation and waited.

General Itskov pushed two ribboned folders towards him across the breadth of the desk.

"In this folder are the dossiers of our Russian physicists involved with the project. Of the four principals one died in the fire. Nevertheless, we have not eliminated him as a conspirator." He opened a blade and cut the ribbon before continuing. "The dossiers have been prioritized for you, Cosarkov. I suggest that you concentrate your efforts on the last two candidates. You will read these documents here, in this room, in front of me. You will remove nothing from the file except what you memorize."

Cutting the second crossed ribboned file, the General continued.

"Here is a new passport for you. It is issued in your name. No complications. It provides you with diplomatic immunity. You will have priority travel and funding, but limited personnel support outside of what this office will provide. Your assignment is to retrieve what was stolen from us. We do not think that the technology has left Moscow yet but we believe that a transfer is imminent. You may negotiate to some level for the return of the technology. If that is not successful, you are authorized to use whatever means you see fit in order to secure its return."

Reaching for the ornate bell on his desk, the old man summoned the appearance of his aide with coffee.

Offering and pouring coffee was Itskov's only interruption of Cosarkov for the next twenty minutes. The only communication between them, the crackling of burning cigarette paper and intermingled smoke.

Time contorted the frame of light surrounding Cosarkov's chair as it moved in shifting proportions on the wall and buttressed the floor behind him until, finally, closing the folder with two hands, Cosarkov offered its return.

"Thank you, sir. I shall begin my assignment immediately. I think that time is not on our side."

Rising to meet him, General Itskov drew his shoulders back and stretched the stiffness from them. He nodded his head in agreement and he extended his hand.

"You are right, Cosarkov. Remember, whatever you need, call me. You must do whatever it takes. Russia's place in world leadership for the next hundred years could be determined by this technology. More than you can imagine rides on your success."

CHAPTER IV

Standing motionless, his legs comfortably apart, crooked to absorb the sideward rocking motion of the subway train, Judd leaned his right shoulder into the pole to stabilize the pull on his body. He watched the others, casually avoiding any direct eye contact, especially with the two girls sitting in the opposite end of the car. He knew that they were in whispered discussion about him. Maybe it was the Brooks Brothers suit, or the wing-tip slip-ons, definitely American, that they found so interesting. Women found him physically attractive and, over the years, it had given him a confidence amongst strangers.

His thoughts moved elsewhere. Much easier to play the game in the Art Gallery adjoining the Hotel where you did not have be paranoid or egotistical to think that every sideward glance was a 'sparrow,' a KGB operative of yesteryears, or an enterprising blackmailer in today's Russia and not just an attractive companion drumming-up foreign currency, living out their circumstance in Moscow.

He shifted the weight of his shoulder-bag and watched the polished aluminum doors opened with quiet efficiency that complimented the system's German origin; Pushkin Square, by count two stops before his hotel. He wondered how they would be after three years of Russian maintenance. Detailed curiosity came naturally to him, it helped focus his attention, it kept his mind occupied. Probably not as quiet as the Tokyo system, but probably not as noisy as the Kowloon Shim Sat Sui line. Their tanks worked, or at least until the first Gulf War although, with Russian crews, who knows how effectively they would have performed! Their rockets worked, but as to the maintenance of oil field equipment such as the line that he was fronting at the Trade Show, he had no idea. A secondary visa application called for him to visit an oil equipment maintenance company in Kazakhstan but, as it had not yet been approved, his thoughts were all speculation. If the visa was not approved, he would confirm his flight and leave in the morning. The trade show had by all accounts, been commercially successful and the Protocol Papers exchanged openly and successfully, in that order. He was looking forward to Prague. Prague, the thought stirred his anxiety. Finally, after so many years. He glanced sideward at the girls who had moved their attention to a young soldier sitting opposite him. The boy was yet unaware of his admirers.

As the train glided forward to operating speed Judd relaxed, accepting his bubbled circumstance as they traveled into the void between stations. The young soldier moved to the rear of the car and engaged the girls in smiling conversation. Judd watched them for a moment before shifting his attention to the images of his fellow commuters reflected in the spotless window panes. Faces of strain and labor that he would not have expected to see in a metropolis, a contrast to the Long Island Express crowd. The tiredness in the faces, around the eyes, was the same, but it was a different kind of tiredness; an expression of mundane survival rather than of New York's emotionally demanding ten-hour work days in the office and two hours of commute time each way, every day.

Unromantic Babushkas with their ever present shopping bags. 'Babushka' the word made universally recognizable by Broadway's Fiddler On The Roof, easy for Americans to pronounce with expression. He could see little redeeming quality for it and wondered if the lack of outward vitality was a circumstance of life, or because their passions had not been caressed since the Great Patriotic War. Probably a little of both. Maybe a Natasha Kinski could only be born to a generation of peace. The distinction of generations was as marked as it was at home. Men who came into their own in the sixties still clinging to the autumn of their lives as if to retain an inner anchor of identity.

'He doubted that Putin's tailor nor Gorbachev's tailor catered to the same comrade-clientele as those on the train, but then again, Gorbachev seemed to be irrelevant at least in Russia, at least still for the time being. The faces of youth seemed more relaxed with themselves than did their elders. He wondered if they cultivated their 'scholarly image' as he had done. A junior year at the Sorbonne dictated by a beige duffel-coat, corduroy slacks, heavy woolen sweater, a pipe and a goatee. The Russians had always honored their writers and their intellectuals, but history seemed to dictate that the first recognition of their success was an embrace of poverty. They weren't at all different from the people at home; struggling to stabilize their individual liberties and material wealth but this would change in two generations of new leadership, if they got their national consciousness together. The myth of the evil empire once presented for local consumption at home, had faded.

Looking back at the military jacket, at the medals on the young soldier, Judd surmised that they were earned in Chechnya. He wondered if the soldier spooked himself every once-in-a-while as he did, years away from the reality of his youth. He felt his face begin to flush, an extra rush of blood moved outward from his chest. Sometimes it was like a penance, sometimes he willed it but the visions and the feelings never got any easier.

The previous night he had walked in Gorki Park with two others from the Trade Show. Walking off the liquor, following the footsteps of

Lee Marvin, as he put it. The air had been cold and crisp, the Northern Lights in relative position as they were at home, leaves patching, quilting the pathways. They had swung their arms and marched in unison to ward away the cold and, as they had approached the crest of a small hillock, panted quietly into single file to engage the narrowing path. He had taken 'point' with no thought to his action as his mind and his eyes began to search out recognizable signs of the path in the shadowed light between the trees and the fallen leaves.

His thoughts were on the darkened ice patches beneath the leaves, slipping on them, stumbling forward. His eyes were on the edge of the path beneath the leaves, falling off it. And then, he was gliding. Step by step. His body one with his mind, focused to bungee-sticks and to the percussion of explosives telling him that he had lost. Moving in balanced animation, he followed the path as it unfolded before him. His cover from the tree lines left to his companions. "Not too far out-front, not too far to where they can't help." He stopped, as suddenly as naturally as he had begun.

A prolonged moment of hesitation, of confusion, and then reality as he looked back down the path. His companions weren't watching the tree lines, they were standing forty feet behind him, hands in their overcoat pockets, in a Moscow Park on a cold winter night, watching him. Waving them forward he had waited, covering his embarrassment by lowering his head and shuffling his feet; a jig of vodka and the moment was forgotten in the laughter by his companions.

After all these years, it was still with him. But he knew that for some reason he liked it, that he brought it on himself. That night, alone, he sought out the companionship of a local 'art lover' from the Gallery. He just needed to hold and to be held; it was a comfort he had not found in his wife for many years, when he needed it most.

The train slowed as it reached the shadowy extreme of the subway platform, diverting the intensity of his thoughts, bringing him back to the moment. He waited in concert with the other passengers for the doors to open. Through the panel windows the station marker-lights passed in slowing succession as the train approached the outer boundaries of the platform. White marble, catacombed pools of reflective light emanating from an unseen height, blurred images of people against a background of bright sterility.

Poised, he moved quickly as the train braked to a gradual, jolting stop and the doors gaped open onto the platform. He fell-in step behind a young couple who, intent on buttoning their coats and adjusting their Italian backpacks, buttressed him towards an exit sign and the surface streets. He lost sight of them to the merging and reforming crowd as his eyes followed the invisible path of an updraft of chilled, recycled air as he reached the first bank of escalators. The escalator moved him upward, opening and expanding the heart of the subway to view.

Monolithic, reflective of the Communist State that built it, the structure lacking the subtlety of personal expression. Maybe it was a huge bomb-shelter doubling as a subway-system as the United States Federal Civic Preparedness Council claimed every time they went before Congress for their budget appropriation. But today, they weren't the enemy, so forget it. He waited for the escalator to slide from under his feet at the apex of its' rise and moved towards the Men's Room discerned by the single gender line that floated in and out of a set of swinging doors one level below the entrance to the Trade and Convention Hall.

A Babushka, uniformed in a heavy woolen coat, scarf, shawl and fingerless gloves patrolled the outer doors, vigilantly sweeping each cigarette-butt that appeared within her designated territory, ignoring those that were discarded over some imaginary line. He watched her and thought of Tamara Press, weightlifter extraordinaire.

Shifting the bag-strap on his shoulder, redistributing the weight, he stopped in front of the double doors, and with deliberation, extinguished his cigarette in an already overfull water-filled container. He looked toward the babushka, but he was unnoticed. Her attention was on the area in front of her broom. Pushing open the plastic veneered covered door he hesitating long enough to reconnoiter, but not long enough to warrant a lingering eye, before moving to an open urinal and unzipped his fly, with both hands held like horse-blinkers and his attention focused on a chip in the white tile grout in front of his navel. He waited for nature to take its course. At his age, it sometimes took longer. A casual glance down verified that all was well at the same time that he heard the forced breathing of a figure, smaller than himself, as it moved to the urinal to his right. Tucking his elbow solidly into the ribbing of his bag, he held it in place, unwilling to casually bump anyone in a Russian Men's Room, especially when both parties were preoccupied. An unnecessary introduction. He looked straight ahead with conscious effort, aware that his neighbor was studying him. Tempted to cast a quick, curious sideward glance at the man, he decided against it. A voluntary smile over a urinal was even less necessary than a nudge with his bag.

Head down, he watched the image of his neighbor in his peripheral vision. The man's naugahyde shoes below the stall divider bespoke their Russian origin, undistinguished, except for their lack of polish. The bottom of the pant legs, exposed under a heavy, molting fur-trimmed coat, had lost any sign of bow-creases. He sensed an urgency, an agitation in the man's demeanor. Perhaps the building of courage for an opening remark. The shuffling stall attendant to his left, preoccupied in his own world wouldn't be of much use to blunt an advance, verbal or otherwise by his neighbor. Looking away, Ethan cut things short and zipped his fly while exiting the same door through which he had entered, without looking back.

On the opposite side of the foyer he lost himself in group of commuters around the public reader boards. His instinct was confirmed as two uniformed men move through the double doors of the Men's Room, followed closely by two others in plain clothes. He did not wait for the conclusion of the scene to unfold but merged into a double line forming at the crossroads platform of the upward moving escalator bank leading up to the Trade Hall entrance. Waiting for the metal steps to extrude to their full configuration, he stepped forward with another. Angling his body backwards, taking in the panorama of the crowded subway platform as it unfolded below his rising perspective, he watched with renewed curiosity as a commotion unraveled outside the Men's Room. A scuffle, the beginning of a protest, the beginning of a pursuit. The uniformed men pushed through the cords of converging commuters, attempting to follow the path of their quarry.

"The little bugger has gotten away from them." From the farthest extreme of the station that he could see, he began to scan backwards, in small blocks, studying, searching the moving figures that formed and blurred and reformed in front of him. His pattern moved closer to the men's room, to the center.

"Okay, okay. Look for the flow; what's not right!" He knew what he was looking for. A patch of silence when you are surrounded by the company of cicadas."

He looked for any sign of the little man moving in the crowd. Nothing! He watched a plain clothed man, blond, standing on a bench, also searching within the flow of the crowd. And then he saw him, he saw the movement of the rabbit.

With quiet deliberation, the man was moving forcibly up the escalator, towards him. Quiet apologies to those who objected to his pushing helped his effort as he squeezed passed and continued climbing, never breaking his eye contact with Ethan.

He thought to turn his back on the advancing figure, to ignore his way out of any entanglement. Instead, he held his position. He did not search for verbal or visual contact with the plain clothed Policeman bruising his way through his fellow citizenry. Instead, he waited for the man to reach him, recognizing a look of quiet desperation, of finality in the man's face. Finality, a feeling he remembered in himself before his last patrol missions in Vietnam so many years ago. April 1st, 1968 and June 10th, 1970. Two tours. Dates he remembered like his children's birth dates. He adjusted the position of his shoulder strap bag, took a deep breath, and waited.

The man halted, one step below and to his right, his presence blocked from his pursuers on the foyer-level by a woman sharing the same step. Ethan followed the man's glance downward in the direction of the foyer, and then he waited.

"You are American!" the man asked rhetorically, turning his attention back to him. "My father knew Americans in the Great War, in Berlin."

He could see the man searching with his eyes for the English and its pronunciation. Nodding his head in acknowledgment of the statement he waited as the man changed his stance, hands outstretched on the running arms of the escalator, his feet spread on two steps, contracting his physical presence as the escalator reached the halfway point of their journey upward.

"From where?"

He watched the perspiration accumulating on the man's forehead and pulled the first of four states that came to his mind.

"Maine."

"My father's friend was from Oregon," the man responded rhetorically with a shrug of apology for his inquisitiveness. "Have you been to Oregon?"

"No," Ethan answered, unwilling to volunteer a conversation as he glanced down to the base of the escalator where he saw the two uniformed Policemen begin their climb. The escalator steps were three deep and the pursuers were finding the obstacle course of business men with briefcases, children, protective parents and others difficult to negotiate.

The man followed his glance to the approaching officers. He made no attempt to move on.

"I want to visit Florida but . . . " he shrugged, returning his attention to the American.

Ethan acknowledged the statement with a silent nod, almost thankful that the approaching Authorities would cut-short any manipulative 'hook' that, under different circumstances, would probably have been pitched to him about now.

"At what hotel you stay?" the man asked, shifting his weight onto his back leg.

Ethan glanced at his inquisitor, ready, if asked his name, to give that of his best friend from fifth grade.

"At the Rossiya." Another lie. It wasn't that he was comfortable at talking with the man, but he was equally uncomfortable with the idea of either volunteering the man's presence to the police or getting involved in something that he could not control. He glanced at the approaching mezzanine landing and then downward to the Policemen who had spied their quarry and were intent on closing-in.

"How many days do you stay in Moscow?"

"Two days, maybe three,"

The man smiled thinly before he looked down again, measuring the progress of his pursuers now forcing their way up the lower extreme of the escalator. Without warning, he sprang upward with a sudden rush that collapsed them both into three women behind them. A moment of confusion between shopping bags and heavy coats, flaying arms, voices and the moving escalator that kept everybody off-balance.

"I'm sorry, Mr. Maine," the man whispered, struggling on top of Ethan and another. The men below were now wrestling in their own collapsed pile five steps below them. Pressing against Ethan's bag the Quarry raised himself up and began climbing towards the sightline of the mezzanine landing above them.

Struggling off his back, Ethan pulled himself to a standing position, not wanting to be drawn and hooked into the approaching escalator grating. Isadora Duncan came to his consciousness, strangulated by a freak accident of rotating mechanical engineering. Turning, he extended his hands to two of the women who had cushioned his fall moments before. He did not have to understand Russian to recognize their verbal irritation and refusal of his offer.

Turning, he retrieved his bag, time enough only to clutch it to his chest and straighten his body against the side of the escalator. Time enough only to clear space for the barging uniformed men who pushed past him unceremoniously. The first raced to intercept the figure in the fir trimmed coat who was attempting to disappear into the crowded Mezzanine above them.

He could hear the intake of breath of the second man as he drew parallel and hesitated. Their eyes locked, for a moment, before the man, looking back at the fallen passengers who began to protest the events to him, resumed his pursuit. Ethan watched the back of the blond head until it disappeared over the top of the escalator as it carried the man to the apex of its cycle. Stepping off himself, he moved towards the first exit he could see, checking for his wallet, his watch and the closures of the two closed zippers on his bag, "Damn, that's all I need, to get dragged into this!" Everything was in its place. With a single motion he swung the bag strap higher onto his right shoulder and retrieved his cigarettes and a matchbook from his overcoat pocket.

Ignoring the Trade Hall doors, Ethan moved towards the nearest exit and open spaces. Exiting at the Marx Prospecks' he walked at a committed pace towards Red Square. His breath was regular and deep by the time he reached the GUM State Department Store complex. The physical exertion a distraction from his thoughts. Arbat Street and dinner were acknowledged and dismissed as he moved past the red bricked walls of the Kremlin towards the Moskvg River. The downward grade of the footpath at the Spassky Gate carried him toward the river and his hotel.

Dismissing the Concierge's greeting with the slight nod of his head he entered the hotel, allowing himself the briefest reconnoiter of the foyer of the hotel as he moved to the front desk.

The atmosphere of the lobby never seemed to change despite the odd-hours in which he had passed through it. A formal staging area in which the starkness of the Scandinavian furniture seemed to stifle the opportunity for intimate conversation. The hotel was frequented mainly by Europeans and he preferred that over the American delegations. Besides, this was his third visit to the hotel and some of the staff recognized him on-sight. It gave him a sense of self-gratification.

With his room key in hand he moved to the Message Desk.

"Good evening, Mr. Judd. I am sorry but I have no messages for you."

The girl's badge stated 'TRAINEE' and Ethan warmed to her diligence.

He raised his eyebrows and smiled. "I am expecting a package, from the Ministry of Resources. When it arrives, would you please see that it is brought to my room immediately!

"I will personally deliver it myself, Mr. Judd," she smiled.

He grinned to himself as he moved to the elevator acknowledging that he was reading more into her response than was there. The package would contain an entry visa for Kazistan, an opportunity to inspect some of the Gulf Resources' oil equipment in the field. A diversion that he would rather not have to fulfill.

From room service he ate in the bath and read his newspaper until, perspiring from the steam, he showered and relaxed onto the bed. He was asleep within minutes.

Awakening to the last vestige of his jet lag several hours later, he reached across the bed as if to relive the memory of his previous night's companion. A sigh began his motion as he lifted back the covers and dressed by the diffused light radiating from the Kremlin through the window in his room. With his pajamas tucked into his slacks and under a jersey, he made his way down to the lobby.

Twilight between shifts, the message desk long since closed, its attendants having moved to their own obligations. There was nothing posted for him on the message board. His confirmation had not arrived.

Inquiry at the front desk also proved negative and, with little thought, he requested that his account be made ready for an early departure in the morning. In his room he packed, his thoughts already in Prague, stirring memories and emotions.

The Airline offices were closed, but he knew that he could secure a standby seat on the first flight to Prague, even on the flight deck if necessary. An American passport and paying for airline tickets or any other considerations in US dollars still had their advantages in certain circles.

His plane departed Sheremetyevo Airport before the eight o'clock Kremlin Honor Guard was changed. It was a clock that Muscovites, otherwise shopworn to the ceremony and the shin-splints of the honor guard, could set their watches by.

CHAPTER V

Cosarkov was uncomfortable from the moment he passed through the barricade at the compound entrance. He did not have to look upwards; he could feel the gray cloud sky, the flat, iron-meshed archer windows that lessened themselves at the oddest, seemingly random placement within the fortressed walls that paralleled his march.

No relief of color nor sound, only his boots on the cobblestones and the thinning veins of rust-stained pipes, skeltered up and down, their beginning and their end intertwined, sucked inward through the surrounding brickwork, faded watermarks the only proof of uninterrupted time.

In twelve years of military service, he had visited Lubiana only twice and this visit would be as secret as the others. The difference now was his badge that identified him as part of the establishment, no longer a supervised 'official visitor,' but one, by association, with the institution itself. His conscience was uncomfortable.

He blocked the sounds of anguish that he sensed, burdened, suspended within the walls. Sounds he visualized, released at the precise moment that a human spirit recognized it was lost to the darker side of its fellow man. Easier to accept the death of the body on the battlefield than to face it here, defenseless. There was no shame in death, no penance nor sorrow, but he was uncomfortable with the thought of valiant death, of valor ignored, locked forever in this damned place.

He cleared the security check in the lobby and walked the three flights of broad banister stairs to the interrogation floor, the dungeon-cell that held his prisoner.

He occupied his mind with the men and women, the architects and the builders, who labored here with creative hands and minds. "Who decided how big the cells should be? Which cells should have windows, and why? How thick did a concrete wall have to be to make it soundproof from screaming lungs to a passer-by on the street below?" He wondered if they discussed the intricacies of such technical details with their wives, their husbands, their lovers, or if they hid their work and wrestled their emotions to sleep every night with unfeeling intercourse.

Childhood stories of dragons and prisoners and dungeons deep in the bowels of the earth came to mind. His psyche told him he should be walking downward, not upward, above the rooftops of surrounding buildings. "Why was the building designed this way?" Thought distracted but did not relieve his uneasiness. "Maybe that's what it was all about! Reality has very little to do with fantasy, yet fantasies distracted the perception of physical reality at every turn of his journey.

He wondered of his responsibility to the prisoner as he signed in at the floor station. Information was his objective. How it was extracted from the man was not his decision. But it was now the preoccupation of his thoughts.

He remembered his battlefield interrogations in Afghanistan where the play of death or survival made everything so much easier to rationalize than behind closed doors, five minutes walk from the subway station, fifteen minutes ride from his apartment, from the bed of his wife of ten years and from their daughter.

He stood formally at ease, it helped disguise his agitation as he waited; no chairs, no convenience, no encouragement to linger until he was led through waves of antiseptic cleaner that flushed from behind the grey environment of concrete walls and closed iron doors.

He did not count the doors as he moved passed them. He did not acknowledge the end of his journey to the young soldier who, halting abruptly, turned and opened an unmarked cell door, an unspoken command to enter. No gesture, no words, no eye contact least a spark of humanity between them acknowledge a collusion of consciousness in such a place.

His eyes confronted the shadow of a man vigilant over a still body strapped to a gurney. The shadow shifted as he entered the room and the door was closed behind him. Cosarkov spoke first. There were no formal introductions.

"Have you killed him?"

"No, Sir, I . . . "

"Then cover him up!" he snapped, gesturing with his chin towards the folded blanket that lay, bathed in focused light, next to a tray of syringes on the table. "I have no interest in your workmanship."

He waited while the Medical Officer, perspiring in his open neck uniform-shirt, his sleeves rolled up, turned his back and, reaching for the blanket, covered the man's legs and torso. The gesture gave Cosarkov time to take in the spatial makeup of the room. His ears screamed at the utter void of sound or reference from outside of the room. No comfort to his unconscious prisoner but, at least, he appeared to be in one piece physically.

He lit his first cigarette of the session without offering one to the interrogator. The gesture did not go unnoticed.

"I do not actually believe that he knows the identity of the courier to whom he passed his information!" the man began.

Cosarkov did not like the man nor his line of work, on principal, but he deferred as calmly as he could to his expertise.

"Why do you say that?"

"He became somewhat unintelligible when it came to describing the courier. That should not have happened with the drug that we, that I, gave him. I have experienced this response before. He began something about his father and a main!"

"What is 'a main'?" Cosarkov asked with his shoulders through his cigarette smoke. "Is it a noun, a place, an object? A horse's mane? The city of Algermain? The man was apprehended in the subway, was he referring to the main train track, to the platform, what was it? He shrugged, "I need more than you have given me!"

The man was visibly frustrated at his failure to produce the results that the military major demanded, but he knew he would find them, soon or later.

"You understand, Major," he began, stepping forward, pro-offering a file as he did so, "sometimes with perscolamine, if the dosage is too great . . . "

"What I understand is that you have miscalculated the dosage that you gave the prisoner and now you must give him a contravening drug before you can begin again!"

The man bit the inside of his lip furiously. There was nothing that he could say.

"How long before you can begin again? Read the file to me," Cosarkov commanded before the Interrogator could respond to his first question. He walked to the unconscious figure and studied the face.

"His name is Lanski, Sir. He is Jewish, from Moscow."

"Émigré status?"

"There is nothing in the file, Sir. His brother was refused an exit visa four years ago, because of the nature of the work that he was involved in for the Rodina."

He ignored the man's attempt to wave his patriotism in their discussion. "And what does the report say about his brother's threat to the Motherland, Doctor?" he asked sarcastically, holding his breath, hoping that the State secret was still a secret.

"Nothing, Sir. Only that the work was classified! I believe that. . ."

Releasing a silent sigh of relief he interrupted, pushing the man again.

"Play your recorded interview with the prisoner, please. There is nothing else in the report that I need to know at this time!"

He lit another cigarette and offered one to his fellow conspirator.

"Skip the preliminaries; just play the part where the perscolamine kicks in."

"Yes, Major, of course." The man smiled, warming to the gesture of the cigarette. "You understand, Sir, with one or two more sessions, I will have all of your questions answered, all the blank pieces filled in. This is only the first session, I know that I will. "

"Yes, thank you," he interrupted, running over the voice of the other as he turned back to the gurney. "Unfortunately, I don't have the luxury of that much time. Please play the tape for me now, without interruption!"

Propping himself against the door, Cosarkov watched the wheels of the cassette, first in unison and then one faster than the other, measuring time, past and present, as the interviewer waited, poised to adjust the volume. His lower back was tightening up; he wanted the interview over with. As the dialog began he dropped his head in concentration and listened to what he knew to be a drug-induced truth. He was still, his visual attention on a spot between his boots.

"Again," he ordered quietly, his concentration still fixed to the concrete floor. He did not understand what he had heard. There was a beginning, volunteered as he would have expected, induced by the drug, but there was no direct answer to the question asked. The technician was good, his inquiry succinct, there should be more, there should be more.

He lit another cigarette as he looked at the mounded blanket that allowed him to know only the head and upturned feet of the prisoner whose words he was absorbing. Words disjointed, separated, transposed onto a celluloid tape by a man with no free will. He knew he was hearing the reality the man perceived but he could not focus the logic! He asked his own question, 'what was true reality in a place like this anyway?' He contemplated the question and waited until the interrogator rewound the proof of his work before he pushed the pack of cigarettes across the blanket.

"Again, please."

The man engaged the tape a second time before he reached for the cigarettes. The flare of the match measured their time before the vocals began again. Cosarkov's mind turned to images of the subway chase as he listened to the words on the tape. Closing his eyes, he listened to the silence of the tape after the prisoner lapsed into his overdosed coma. There was something, something there, but he could not recognize it.

Opening his eyes, he looked through the light and shadow to his prisoner, then to his witness, expressionless. The technician continued to perspire, his cigarette smoldered, untouched between his outstretched fingers; he seemed to be holding his breath, his body riveted, afraid to disturb the concentration in the room. He waited for Cosarkov to continue.

"Again!" His one-word command began the procedure over for a third time. The technician glanced nervously at the tape and then fleetingly at the prisoner before he turned to rewind the cassette.

That was it!

"Enough!" Cosarkov said, standing upright. He recognized the missing puzzle piece. "It will not be necessary! Have the prisoner remanded to my custody. There will be no need for further interrogation, at least not tonight!" Reaching for the doorknob, he refused the American Marlboro cigarettes that the man retrieved for him, pushing them back as a gesture.

"You have been most helpful, thank you." The comment was uncalled for, but then again, he did not know when he might run into the man in the future, when he might need him.

Cosarkov moved quickly through the security checks and out of the building and into his waiting car. Subtle waves of relief washed over his shoulders as he distanced himself from the prison. Formulating his telephone report, he dialed the unlisted number. The phone rang twice.

"General, good morning. This is Andre Cosarkov." From a new pack he lit a cigarette and waited for a response, allowing the older man at the other end of the phone connection time to struggle to alertness from what he perceived had been a deep sleep.

He wondered if the phone was on the left or the right side of the bed. He envisaged the old man leaning on one elbow, his left, squinting at his alarm clock for the time, running his freehand through his silvered hair.

"Yes, General, I know that it is only five o'clock. I am sorry to have woken you, but you did tell me to telephone you when there was progress to report!" His voice was edgy, but he was tired and besides, better to get some understanding with his new Commanding Officer now rather than later. He continued without pause.

"I am fairly certain that the information has been passed before we apprehended the suspect, General . . . " He listened, recognizing that the conversation would be methodically drawn out by the General's style of question and answer. "No, Sir, we do not know in what form it was passed." He was feeling as irritable as the old man. "But I believe that it was passed to an American, and I also think that I have seen him!" He allowed his statement to sink in. "Yes, General, here in Moscow. I will visit with Central Services when they open this morning, General, o verify where this American is staying . . . Yes, I will telephone you with any progress . . . No, General, the prisoner has not been fully interrogated, there were certain complications. I have had him remanded into my custody . . . Yes, General, I know that the prisoner is my responsibility. General, I am at my destination. I must go . . . Yes, General, goodbye, General."

He was impatient to lose himself in his own reality as the driver slowed the car to the sidewalk in front of his apartment building. He hoped that the old man's fuzziness from the early morning call would temper the memory of his abruptness, but he did not need to be reminded about his prisoner. He was emotionally tired. No excuse for his irritability but, at this point he really did not care. What he wanted was a shower, to cleanse his body, to wash the touch of the prison from his soul and then to make love with his wife. To draw himself back into the world of the living, touching, knowing. All of this and breakfast in two hours, before another day.

CHAPTER Vl

Prague

The Metropol, a lovers' walk from cobbled Wenceslaus Square. Her hotel. Eiderdown quilts, hot cocoa and toast at two o'clock in the morning. Breakfast in bed.

He had booked the same room. A gesture to retrace something missing from his life for many unrecognized years. He had experienced it, known it with her. He did not expect to find it within the confines of the bedroom suite, but it was his starting point.

He wanted to see her again though she was not the heart of the voice that called him back. Years ignored. But he was here now and his first telephone call, confirming his arrival, committed his decision to return to Prague.

"Janos? This is Ethan!"

He wondered if they would find the same openness, the friendship that they had enjoyed before sixty-four uninterrupted seasons of separation and sporadic family Christmas cards, far from their student days in Paris. He listened to Janos' voice, trying to gleam a sense of him physically. Strong, distant, more formal than he would have hoped for, but none less than he could have expected. The consummate diplomat! Ambassador Vallic! Graying temples, horn rim glasses, wedding band, her wedding band.

"Yes, Janos, I've made reservations at the Septieme, for eight-thirty . . . No, no, thank you, the Septieme will be fine . . . Okay then . . . and . . . okay, good, then I'll see you both at eight-thirty."

He wondered idly how true his friendship really was, how true his smile. His eyes would tell when they met. The formality of Janos' answer made him uncomfortable but it would not change his mood nor his need.

Showered, in a holding pattern in the hotel bathrobe, he placed an eight o'clock call through the Hotel operator to the Varshava Hotel, Moscow while room service set his table. Undisturbed, he ate cross-legged on the bed. With the *Herald Examiner* spread he read until, oblivious to the passage of time, he slept, to rest his body, to wander in his emotions.

The shrill of the telephone jump-started his body again.

Nine o'clock, Moscow time. He picked the phone up after the third ring.

"Mr. Judd, your call to Moscow is on the line. Go ahead, please."

"This is Ethan Judd, I am calling from Prague," he stated with deliberation, hoping that the announcement of an international call would encourage the Hotel Operator not to put him on hold. "Please connect me to Mr. Robert Matson in room seven-two-four."

"Please wait, Sir." he was unsure if he had been put on hold, or if he had lost the connection. He could hear the flow and ebb of people on the hotel street front below, measuring his time as he waited.

"Hello!"

"Hi, Bob!"

"Ethan!" the voice exclaimed. "Where the hell are you?"

He had shared three days at the Trade Show with the man who had been his unwitting guardian while he completed his assignment. There was anxiety in the man's voice, but he did not like being questioned in such an abrupt manner. He answered the question with a question.

"Are you alright, Bob? I'm sorry that I left this morning without calling you but I didn't want to wake you so early!"

"No, that's alright. Look, what happened in your room last night?"

"What do you mean?"

"Well, I went to get you for breakfast just before nine and your room was a bloody shambles. Everything torn-up. The Police were there and some of the hotel staff. Everybody seemed pretty pissed-off! I didn't know if you had left without paying your bill, or if you had one hell-of-a night, or if you had been arrested. A little 'spekulatsiya' on the side!" Mason laughed at his own pronunciation.

Ethan did not react to the feigned brevity about black marketeering. In today's Moscow everything was available. On another occasion, he might have let Matson conjure his own assumptions about his sexual escapades, but not today. He was taken-aback by the image of destruction. He could feel the blood rushing to his throat. He struggled to control his voice.

"Are you kidding?" He hesitated, recalling his movements. "Nothing, when I left this morning at six everything was fine!"

"Well it ain't now! I guess that one of the hotel girls told the Police that you were traveling today. When they asked me if I knew where you were, I told them that you had plans, but that I didn't know where you were or where you would be staying! Where are you anyway?"

"Prague. I didn't hear from the Ministry so I decided to push my schedule up one day. I don't have to be in Paris for another couple of days and so I decided to visit some old friends of mine here." He disliked having to justify his movements but volunteered the information. "I wonder if someone in the hotel thought that I was leaving for the Show and decided to burglarize the room?"

"I don't know, Ethan, but at least you're alright. I don't think that anything else has to be done about it. Would you like me to ask the American Embassy people here to contact the Police to make sure that everything is okay?"

"Yeah, you're right, Bob. I would appreciate that." He felt obliged to thank Matson for his concern. "Look, I'm going on to Paris before I go to London. I'd like to take you and your wife for dinner or something next time I get to Chicago!" It was a commitment he would probably never keep but Matson seemed genuinely pleased by the gesture as they ended the conversation.

Somber, he watched himself shave, recreating emotions, colored thoughts of the burglary until the possibilities of the incident and the telephone call were exhausted. Dressed for dinner, he moved towards another reality, the Old-Town District and his 'Septieme.'

A chance to recapture a warmth in his heart, a memory, an expectation forever new. She had brought him here. She had made love with him in the Metropol. Mitriann.

The vividness of their meeting never faded from him. The drive across the Hungarian border, the wedding of her youngest brother.

He had seen her at the campsite, daughter of a Romani ri, greeting relatives arriving from four continents for the wedding.

Made welcome by her family, he had been content to stay close to their encampment, watching the preparations while Janos, his host, his friend, visited other members of the family and their kampanias.

Janos was not Gypsy himself, but it had been accepted that she might marry outside of her people and from all accounts Janos had been accepted in that role.

Attended by an ever-changing number of children Ethan had

enjoyed his time. Adults avoided any open acknowledgment of his presence, but he knew that he would be introduced, and his relationship established when the time was right. He remembered.

He remembered a moment of quiet as he closed his eyes, his chin upon his chest, his body pressed to a knotted olive trunk. He remembered a shadow, cast upon his body, separating him from the sun as it filtered through the laden branches of his canopy. He remembered the beads of perspiration under his shirt that moved then halted their journey on his torso. He remembered raising his head slowly, painfully, the stiffness in his neck giving way grudgingly, breathing the deep presence of musk.

He remembered the confusion of his mind, forcing it to consciousness. With fingertips he had massaged away the droplets of perspiration that stung beneath his eyelids. He had stretched before blinking in the world that was her presence. Her eyes, an erotic magnetism that drew him in, that captivated him, breathlessly, from the first. She was the most beautiful woman he had ever encountered.

That night, when the musicians appeared and the wine began to flow, she had danced by the light of the flames and he knew that she danced for him. The violins played and she danced until the sweat ran down her face and, overcome by the Tokay, he was lost in her rhythm.

And now, he visited the Septieme, a moment to prepare before he would visit her and Janos again. A voyeur, reliving moments of intimacy, naked, unthreatening. Excitement tinged with guilt for his relationship with Janos. He was no longer jealous of her husband. Sometimes he wanted to be but too much time had passed to keep the emotion fresh and compelling. The emotion that excited him for a time could not be sustained. It had faded, neutralized by his acknowledgment, his knowing that he no longer shared her intimacies; but once it had made him feel alive.

The restaurant, a remnant of Central European fabric leftover from yester-years . Its only external announcement a heavy-rubbed brass '714' woven into and above the outer defense of wrought iron gates, three guided steps below the pavement level.

It had survived since Mitterrand's War, a rendezvous for the discreet. A place where food and wine were indulged as an act of foreplay. Its lasting reputation stamped during the early thirties by the avant-garde of Germany's Artists and Hitler's military who set the stage before the sexual eroticism of Europe shifted its center to New York. The restaurant had thrived under the occupation of the Germans and absorbed the deliverance of the Soviets with equal goodwill.

He had been relaxed and comfortable there. The attention to detail by the staff, the tapestries, the carpet-rugs scattered, layered, absorbing all but the most muffled of private conversations and the occasional sound of laughter and crystal; moving candlelight, beacons on each of the tables that drew the room together. It was an atmosphere that had unribboned his heart.

But the feeling had changed. The ranks of older waiters was thinner, replaced by younger men more simpatico with the metamorphose that the restaurant had undertaking. Demonstrations were planned for the following night in Wenceslaus Square, a celebration of the rebirth of the Republic and the staff seemed pre-occupied, cognizant of the shift in political tastes and clientele that they could expect given the upheavals that whirled about them on the other side of the medieval doors that secured their existence.

The intimacy of the room was commanded by the white table-clothed tables and ambient light, reflected through wall-to-wall plate-glass of the French doors, forced by a wrought-iron electric chandelier that drew his eyes to the patio-entrance. Hidden light bulbs streamed weakened shadows onto the floor. The music, soft, rhythm and blues, tapping out the embrace of American communications. The restaurant had changed.

Seated, he took in the single entrance, following it to the smooth marble floor, worn to noticeable paths, but giving up no secrets of its past. Magenta walls, continuous except for an indiscernible mirror reflecting only to the patio tables. The room, scattered with petunias, allocated and bundled in glass, a gesture of the proprietress. It still held emotion for him but he worried how they, how she would accept the restaurant. Like their circumstances, it was different. His heart was excited, too late to worry, too late, too late. Sliding, relaxed in the wall seating, facing outward, he waited for them, for her, to arrive.

Two women and a man. A young couple and a friend. A married couple and a single friend, her friend. A provincial friend. The couple, showing her their intellectual discovery of the city. He watched them.

The man was uncomfortable with his role or was he just bored. A stranger himself, other than to the city's street grids. His wife, portraying a calm confidence and ownership rights of her surroundings and of her husband. Both deferring to the older generation of Bohemia.

The stranger, unwilling to allow herself the pleasure of relaxing to enjoy the experience of her surroundings. Her hair, beautiful, thick, cut to her ears, shiny, not yet dulled by the hardness of the city's tap water.

Ethan wanted to catch her eye, to smile, to let her know that she would do just fine. Mephisto Waltz, until, as abruptly as he had centered to the three, they departed. He began the process over. Waiting. Waiting for Janos. Waiting for Mitriann.

Mitriann approached softly, in the wake of the maître d' towards his table. She was alone. Janos, where was Janos? His pulse quickened as she hesitated, for but a moment as she recognized his presence. She smiled across the distance of the tables.

Rising, moving towards her, he thrilled at her presence. What to say, after so many years! His heart had never changed, but where was his justification; so much time, so much time. It had been easy to kindle his love from a distance and now he watched the distance dissolve as she moved towards him. It was easy to draw out his emotions when he was alone, he enjoyed the thirst, the longing for her, memories of her words, his feelings and tears, his awareness of himself, as a man, as a man in a relationship that held no tomorrow.

And now, he took a deep breath, unsure, hesitant. How to greet her. Janos, where was Janos? Did he dare to acknowledge her differently without his presence? Assumptions, hesitation, uncertainty. So much time, so much time. To hold her hands, to touch her lightly on both of her cheeks, to inhale the fragrance of her presence; to touch the inside of her wrist with his lips, to guide her gently to the table! What to say, how to say it. Seventeen years and now everything was dissolving except his consciousness of what her memory had meant to him for all those years.

Ethan stopped, waiting as the maître d' reaching the final passage of his formal escort, stepped aside, his head inclined towards Mitriann in sublimation, his accompaniment complete.

Mitriann moved towards him, measured steps, her hands hidden, caressed by the ermine draped over her arms. Black on black silk. He followed the gentle slope of her shoulders to her collarbone and upwards to her earrings, to her face. All else was forgotten when he reached her eyes. He felt their sparkle. His smile told her of his feelings.

He reached for her hands as she offered them to him, low and outstretched. He felt her holding on, matching his pressure, squeezing in return as he imparted his excitement.

"Hello, Ethan," she smiled, her eyes mirroring his, lessening the distance between them before she passed her coat to the deferring arms of the maître d', "I had almost forgotten how good your smile made me feel!"

Truth or sarcasm, grin or grimace, he did not care. Her voice surrounded his heart. His emotions welled, fracturing his voice, blurring his vision. He dared not blink lest he betray his tears. His emotion was real. It was enough, even for a time unknown.

And she, acknowledging his emotion, sort the depth of his eyes, as if to verify what she needed to see, before gently releasing his hand. Smiling softly over her sealed lips, alluring, never imparting or inferring the meaning of their posture, she moved behind the table and waited for him to draw her chair. It was only her eyes that he understood; all else was still a fascination of mystery.

He did not speak. It was the only way to control his excitement, as he moved next to her, drawing her chair, catching for but a moment the subtle tint of auburn in her hair, drawn high above her ears. A glitter of light telegraphed through her earrings. He was drawn to her, drawn to her closeness. Leaning over her shoulder, Ethan inhaled the fragrance of her body as she moved around him and into the chair.

Recognizing his action, unspoken, she inclined her head backwards and smiled. He took in the full length of her neck and shoulders that molded to the gentle curve of her fitted top as he moved around her and rested on the edge of his chair. He studied her. He knew that Janos was not coming and he recognized, for a fleeting moment, how different their meeting would be if he was sitting between them. Sighing, he inhaled her presence; the gentle creases that showed at the corner of her eyes, that framed her silent lips, the sculptured eyebrows that reinforced the delicate curvature of her face. Every motion reinforced the consciousness of her image in his memory. But it was her eyes that he lay with in gentle caress. He followed their sparkle deeper and deeper until, in his heart, he could bear his own silence no longer.

"You are beautiful," he whispered, and she watched with seriousness the tear that glazed along the creases of his eyes. She waited.

Ethan smiled without embarrassment. It said what he could not say with words. The brightened sparkle in her eyes was the only outward change in her response.

"I have no words for you, Mitriann!" he shrugged.

She did not speak, but looked away, towards the approaching waiter. Waiting for the interruption to end they listened absently to the motion of the wine as it was poured, raged and then calmed within its surround.

Mitriann lifted her goblet from the table, inviting him to do the same, to meet her halfway.

"Then don't say anything until you are ready," she grinned, "there is no rush between us!"

Twisting his torso sideways in his chair, he responded softly to her. "If you mean that it has been seventeen years since we were lovers, you are right!"

Her face lightened with a mischievous smile around her closed lips. This was the smile that had beguiled him, that drew him to her, he could feel it again.

"Your time has been good to you," he opened gently with a smile matching hers, still circling her face with his eyes, absorbing the femininity, the erotica of her age.

She held the goblet at her lips and frowned mockingly at him.

"If you mean that young men don't look at me anymore, I'm not so sure about that. Besides," she smiled, "is that what you came to tell me?"

He watched her lips as she pursed them to the crystal. Unprovoked fantasy, to reach them with his own. He knew her eyes followed his as he looked to the table linen, smiling at the presumption of his thoughts, smiling at the open flights of fantasies when he was with this woman.

"What?" she asked, lowering her glass, smiling at him in return. The moment of whatever hesitancy there was between them vanishing as she did so.

"A thought, Mitriann, my own, but perhaps it is why I came, or part of it at least." He volunteered with a frown, a roll of his right shoulder. "I am unsure, but I have wanted to talk. I have wanted to talk with you for a long time."

"And what about Janos, Ethan! My husband, your friend, have you wanted to talk with him also?"

Drawing his lips inward, he shook his head in the negative before he answered.

"I don't know if it's so much to talk as to reach an understanding. To know that, in some way, our relationship still continues."

"You know why he did not come tonight?"

"Betrayal!"

"No, Ethan," she smiled, raising her eyebrows, "you assume too much. My relationship to Janos is open, nothing is held from the past. He did not come so that this would be your time with me. He knew that it is necessary. That it has been necessary for these many years. Besides, would you talk like this now if Janos was here with us?"

The frown line above the bridge of his nose bespoke of the intensity of his thoughts as he shrugged.

"I don't know, Mitriann! Differently I'm sure. Not as intense, perhaps not as openly, not as honestly."

"What do you mean by honest, Ethan?"

"Well," he began, leaning on his elbows over the table, raising his eyes to meet here, "perhaps things would have been left to feelings, unspoken, left to assumptions; half answers, half resolutions left for perhaps another time."

"Another eighteen years?" she smiled, reaching for his hand. "I'm sorry, Ethan. That was not fair."

He did not answer. He knew that her perception was clear. She had always demanded his honesty, to her and to his own thoughts. It had been hard for him to keep that clarity when he was younger but he felt it more and more as he grew older. Perhaps this was what he had come to Prague to tell her. But whether it was the explanation of a new opportunity or of a closure he did not know.

Mitriann's silence encouraged him to continue.

"Many times I have thought to visit with you. Sometimes my need, my emotions would almost overwhelm me with a longing, to touch, to know, to talk, with you."

"Then why didn't you come?" she asked without rebuke.

He lowered his eyes and shrugged. "I don't know! Family, a wife, children finding the time, another complication." But he did know and he felt the conviction rising, that he was not being honest with her. He felt a sweet panic to voice what he felt inside his heart before the moment was lost.

"No, I do know, Mitriann," he said, looking up, meeting her eyes, "I didn't know how to react to you and Janos. Janos was my friend, is still my friend, I hope, but it was you whom I would have come to visit. I couldn't do that to Janos!"

"And so you did nothing, for all of these years! What about me, Ethan, did you think of me? Or were your thoughts only of yourself?

He had not thought of it in those terms. His emotions surged through his chest. He could not give her a one-word answer.

"Sometimes, at the oddest times, in the oddest places, I still feel your presence, somewhere outside my peripheral vision, but surrounding my heart. An echo, sometimes from a void, empty, far away, far away. Sometimes I knew it was you. Sometimes I didn't know who it was."

He closed his eyes and rested his chin on his folded fists before continuing. "It was such a lonely call, Mitriann. It called from a depth of my being that I chose to ignore for so many, many years. It called from a place of love but I never did anything about it!"

Feeling his vulnerability she reached out and touched his forearm with her fingertips. He did not pull back.

"Why didn't you, Ethan, if it was that strong?"

Clenching his jaw, he felt a deeper moment of truth drawing upward within and around him.

"Why didn't you come, Ethan? If you knew where that call was from!"

He took her hands, accepting, trusting that she would not judge him by his inactions, his avoidance of himself, but by where his heart had led him to today.

Casting across his face, she nodded, exhaling in recognition of the inevitable finality of where their words would end.

"Ask me, Ethan, ask me now."

Drawing on all of his resolve, he began to feel the courage of his truths, hidden, avoided for so long. He wanted desperately to share his inner secrets, without fear, with love, to another human being. He was afraid of what he knew was the truth, afraid of unknown complications and realities. He was afraid to question her and yet he knew that he would never find his peace if he did not face himself here. He was afraid and yet he had never felt so alive.

"Then I will tell you, Ethan. I will tell you what your heart is asking. Samera is your daughter."

Closing his eyes he grimaced, the heightened pounding in his heart drawing off the wrenching edges of his emotions that surged to overwhelm him. Relief. Release from an emotional expectation that he had compounded and carried for so many years. Relief of having followed the voice that spoke to him from his heart; he was doing it. The beginning of a forgiveness of himself, a closure with Mitriann, the end of something, the beginning of something new. The end of quiet for a young woman whom he had never met, who was his daughter.

Mitriann was silent and still, her eyes never left his face. She watched and waited.

In his heart Ethan moved towards her and towards his daughter, towards the voice that cried out from the darkness. He drew them to him, mingling tears, for himself and for Mitriann and for the daughter he had never known.

Opening his eyes he met Mitriann's look, drawing her to smile with him, each recognizing that they had, together, completed a passage. He had invited change and she, in return, had moved him towards it. No thought, no fear of consequences, only the open truth of their hearts, for themselves and for each other.

He spoke quietly, fighting the constriction, the choking sensation that manipulated his vocal cords. "I cannot speak what I feel in my heart,

Mitriann, I don't have the words, but I know that you are right. You have always forced me to address myself honestly."

"It is all that I ever asked for, Ethan."

She watched him rock, gently, almost imperceptibly, comfortable with himself. She watched him smile.

Moving forward on her seat, relieving the tension of her body, she grinned. "Well, then I'm happy for you and for Samera as well."

He nodded, thinking about a cigarette for the first time that evening.

"Does Samera know that I am her father?"

"Yes," she responded with the slightest of a furrow on her forehead and surprise in her voice. "I felt no reason not to tell her the truth!"

He watched her, without reaction, trying to picture a time and place when she would have taken Samera aside, a void of time that would have changed his daughter's self-image, her perception of who she was, forever. His thoughts tumbled with those of his own childhood, mirrored mistakes, unprovoked damage, recognized only by the child who remained silent, carrying the burden to his own children.

"And Janos?" he asked without finishing his question.

"And Janos, what?" she asked, blunting his half question, forcing him to remain honest to himself and to her.

"I'm sorry, Mitriann," he nodded, recognizing his avoidance. "Does Janos know that I am Samera's father?"

"Yes, of course he does," she stated, almost running over his words before he had finished. "I could not have married him with an untold truth!"

He marveled at her emotional honesty, the clarity of her self-image that he heard and saw in her face. He wondered where the confidence of such inner strength came from in a person. He felt it, every once-and-a-while, but not like this.

He thought of Janos, how much he must love her, how hurt he must have been when she told him that Samera was not his birth child. He tried to gauge his own feelings of acceptance and love towards the child of another, wondering how he would have reacted if their roles had been reversed. He wondered at Janos, recognizing the strength of the man, realizing why he had not accompanied her tonight.

"Why did you not tell me, Mitriann?"

"For the same reason that, if you suspected, why did you not call and ask me if I was pregnant Our time together was short, Ethan, but not that short!"

The height of the cold war, an American and a Czech citizen. He had clung to that rationale, but he knew that he had not been honest. He could not answer her with words, but only the tacit raise of his eyebrows.

"When did you tell Samera?"

"The first time that she asked me!" Mitriann answered, watching Ethan's silence.

"Ethan," she smiled, emphasizing the 'you,' drawing his attention back, "if you want answers, you must first ask the questions. I am not going to assume anything. I am not going to make this easy for you."

"I know, Mitriann, I know," he responded gently, feeling her rebuke for the first time. "It is my truth to understand your relationship with Samera and Janos, but it is also my truth to understand my relationship with you."

She paused for the longest moment and he waited, with open intensity, telling himself that he would accept whatever words she gave him, accepting whatever impact they would have on his future. He listened to her words, flowing, without remorse or excitement to this moment, flowing from eighteen years of silent formulation.

"I love you, Ethan, I always have. But I gave you up a long time ago. For my sake, for Samera's sake," she gestured with her shoulders before she continued, "that you are here today, I don't know how I feel. But I know that there will never be anything between us again."

Reaching for her hand, interrupting her, recognizing her vulnerability for the first time that night, tenderness urged his words.

"Mitriann, please, don't say any more tonight. It is enough that you came and that we have talked. I don't know what my future will be but I would like Samera to consider being a part of it, somehow, if she would like." He frowned, squeezing the palm of her hand as he continued, "I don't know what that means for my relationship to Janos, to you, but I know that I want to try, not to make up for what was never lost to me, but for what I have found. When my work is finished, I would like to meet again, to talk again with you. To ask both you and Janos if I can talk with Samera, to visit with her!"

"That decision is not mine nor is it Janos's to make, Ethan," Mitriann frowned. "That decision belongs to Samera alone, but," she hesitated, her smile leading her words, "despite what she says, I think that she is a little bit curious about you!"

Smiling, he reached with his free hand for his wine glass, offering it up as a toast.

To the other patrons of the restaurant, the touch of their glasses was but another crystal toll to the god of all lovers.

CHAPTER VIl

"Mr. Judd, Mr. Judd!" the white-cuffed hand beckoned as it waved its way past the congested lobby counter, anxious to make contact, arresting Ethan's movement towards the elevator. "Mr. Judd, my name is Laslow. I am the Night Manager of the hotel." Deprecating, the man continued, the palms of his hands pressed together, downcast as if in supplicating. "Mr. Judd, we are so sorry for the disturbance. I have taken the liberty of moving you tonight, to the Duchess Room and, of course, your entire stay with us is complementary. We . . . "

"Excuse me!" Ethan frowned, physically tired, emotionally elated, watching a uniformed police man moving towards him at a distance behind the hotel manager.

"Mr. Judd," the manager continued, lowering his voice, his stress exaggerating the feminine gestures of his hands. "There has been a burglary, in your room! The police are here to investigate. Naturally, I have taken the responsibility of ... "

"Mr. Judd!" a voice interrupted rhetorically behind him, hesitating until Ethan turned to face him. "I am Inspector Albrecht with the Prague Constabulary," The man sighed, the uneven ends of his oversized mustache, the oversized-coat reinforcing the tiredness in his demeanor. Raising a smile, he continued, "My silent assistant behind you is Officer Mikealic. He will accompany us to your hotel room."

Acknowledging the introduction, Ethan turned to encompass both men in his sight as the Manager, ignored, moved away, diplomatically out of earshot.

The gesture of his passport, held loosely in the Inspector's hand, an unbreakable bond between them, was not lost to Ethan as they moved towards the staircase. The older man took his arm as two old friends would walk in the intimacy of familiarity.

"We would ask you to tell us what is missing. To give us a statement, for our records."

Looking down at the plodding roundness of the man's shoulders, Ethan bit the inside of his lip.

"At what time did this happen, Inspector?" I have been away from the room for less than three hours!"

Yes, we know when you left the hotel," the man exclaimed, his deliberate attention on the polished tips of his shoes as if willing them up the carpeted stairs. "It seems that the night maid interrupted your intruder as she was about to prepare your room for the evening."

"Were there any other rooms broken into?"

Albrecht ignored the question as they reached the guarded hotel room. The Policeman raised his eyebrows and hesitated, an unspoken command for Ethan to enter the room first. Drawing a cigarette from his coat pocket, Albrecht studied the American's face as it moved past him, disturbing the air around the match that the uniformed officer pro-offered. He followed Ethan into the room.

"I am embarrassed for our fair city, Mr. Judd. Embarrassed that such lawlessness should be ours." Moving towards the bathroom, verifying the emptiness of its silence, the older man continued. "Since these past few years, so much as affected the fabric that is our nation. With our march towards democracy and entry into the E.U., so too has come an increase in the displacement of our citizens and the crimes and problems that seem to so natural to the capitalist system and to the human condition."

Ethan took in the displaced confusion that was his room. He did not respond. He could feel the disrupted energy of his belongings as they had hit the floor, confusing their orderly repose. The Orvis travel case, upside-down, separated along its base, open, violated. The dresser drawers, ajar, empty, reinforcing the shortness of his intended stay. The mattress, its fall broken by the pillows, balanced awkwardly against the bed frame. Ethan thought of Moscow, he thought of Mitriann, of Samera, he was tired.

"I ask you to tell us what is missing, Mr. Judd," Albrecht asked, moving to the end of the bed, exposing a knitted cardigan that seemed appropriate to his turtle like demeanor as he removed his overcoat. "It is a routine matter, but one that involves a foreign national and, therefore, must be reported."

Ethan shook his head, relieved at the statement, thinking of the expenditure of manpower and effort required to balance what seemed the insignificance of the act committed. "Outside of my watch and my ring, both of which I am wearing," he began, lifting his hands with his fingers and wrists expose, "the only other items of value would be two pairs of gold cufflinks on my shirts and ten thousand dollars worth of traveler's cheques that I keep hidden in my travel bag, and then my carry bag . . ."

Dividing the statement, the uniformed officer moved to the open closet and lifted out the bundled shirt hangers. He ran his hands under the plastic wrap that surrounded the shirts, verifying the presence of the cufflinks.

"Please check that your money is still in place, Mr. Judd." And where are your other bags?"

Ethan dropped to his knees next to the overturned carry-on case and reached into an unseen crevice. He produced the folded traveler's cheques which he held up to Albrecht for verification.

"There is only one travel case, Inspector. It was here when I left. My passport, which you now have, along with some business papers were left in the hotel safe." Standing, he produced his wallet, pocketing the traveler's cheques. "I have my wallet and, other than that, I am carrying nothing of value!"

Albrecht picked up the fallen lamp that lay, obstructing the dog-eared corner of the mattress, crumpled by its own weight on the carpet, and deposited it on the night-table.

"Is this your bag, Mr. Judd?"

Raising himself to his feet, Ethan moved around the end of the stylized bedposts, confronting the leather shoulder bag that was exposed as the uniformed officer leveraged the mattress back onto the bed.

"Yes it is, Inspector."

"Please go through it for me!"

Papers were strewn on the floor, mixed with receipts, paperclips, business cards, matchbooks, a chocolate bar. He shrugged.

"Inspector, there is really nothing here of value except to me! I don't see that anything has been taken."

"Well, then my work is done for the night. I am not hopeful that we will apprehend the culprit, at least not tonight!" Albrecht sighed, moving towards the door. "I must say that you have taken this unpleasant incident most calmly, Mr. Judd!"

Ethan thought again of Moscow. "What else is there to do, Inspector? Nothing was stolen but my time!"

"Somehow this whole thing does not feel right, Mr. Judd," the older man shrugged, entering the broad expanse of the hallway.

Deliberately, quietly, he took in the scene of the crime before he locked his eyes in earnest with those of the victim.

"Still, perhaps you were lucky and the maid interrupted the crime before any damage could be done!"

Ethan moved into the doorway, breaking the man's study.

"I understand that you will be leaving us tomorrow!"

"Yes, I leave for Paris in the morning."

"Paris!" Albrecht whispered softly, raising his eyebrows, shifting their irregularity, twisting the ends of his mustache as if in remembrance of some long-past love affair. "Then you will be needing this," he said, offering up the passport. "Unless you wish to file a formal complaint, in which case I would have to ask you to remain here in our beautiful city for another day or two!"

Ethan reached for his passport. "No Inspector, I do not want to file a formal complaint. It would seem that you are overworked as it is!"

"You are right, Mr. Judd," he grinned, "but such is the life of a humble policeman!"

CHAPTER VIII

Ethan was unaware of the figure that moved towards him as he idly watched the blue tail of the British Airways 320 glide across the lower expanse of the terminal window in front of him. He was absorbed in his thoughts, reliving the restaurant scene with Mitriann, watching her through the back window of the tax as he had stood on the curb outside of the restaurant until the vehicle turned and she was lost to his sight. She had not looked back.

"Excuse me, I could not help but notice, did I see you at the Metropol this morning?"

Surprised by the interruption Ethan took in the athletic figure that filled out the El Al uniform. Except for an elderly couple, doting over each other with tea, they were alone in the lounge.

"Yes, I was staying at the Metropol," he nodded, removing his reading glasses. In the First Class Air France lounge, he knew that she did not work there.

"I understand that there was some excitement in the hotel last night!" she said, the gentle curve of her shoulders turned frontal to him.

"Actually, it was my room that was burgled!" he exclaimed, registering the energy that her presence gave so freely.

"Ah, so you were the American!" she exclaimed, sitting down opposite him, smiling, volunteering him to continue. "Were you hurt? Did you catch the burglar? Did you lose anything?"

"No, nothing and I was not there at the time. It seems that the house maid interrupted whoever it was before he or she could take anything!"

"Lucky," she smiled, "I hope that the hotel took good care of you after that!"

"They were most apologetic," he said, catching the attention of the Lounge Staff who moved his table. "I was about to order coffee, would you care to join me?"

"Cappuccino, thank you."

He ordered and waited for her to speak, taking in her fragrance as she leaned across the table, depositing her handbag against his overcoat, draped across the chair between them. She caught him staring and smiled in recognition.

"What?" she questioned, "what are you grinning at?"

His face broadened into a smile.

"At you."

She held his eyes beyond the obvious and pursed her lips. "I like it when you smile," she said, letting go.

Ethan looked down at the newspaper in front of him, a little taken back by her statement, a little taken back by her boldness. He did not having an answer for her.

The arrival of coffees gave them both pause.

Leaning forward, he looked studiously at her lips.

"You have two different coloured lipsticks on!" he stated rhetorically.

It was her turn to blush.

"Not many men would notice that!"

"I did," he smiled, feeling the liberty of her approval to surround himself with her visual presence.

The moment lingered as she held his eyes again until he broke the intensity that bound them.

"My name is Ethan Judd."

"Hello, Ethan," she responded in mock seriousness, offering her hand long enough for him to feel a rush of sensuality run through his fingertips. "My name is Laxmi Cohen."

He relaxed his pressure from her hand and reached for his coffee, covering his awkwardness, rolling her name rhythmically over his tongue. He looked across at the couple preparing to board their aircraft, the woman straightening the man's collar as he stood patiently in front of her.

Laxmi followed his gaze and they smiled in recognition of the intimate affection.

He wanted to continue the conversation, to draw her eyes back to his, a turn of her head back to him, to explore the crescent eyebrows, the darkness of her eyes.

"Laxmi, it is a beautiful name. What does it mean?"

It is an Indian name, it means money, and you pronounce it as if there was a letter 'a' after the 'x.'"

He pronounced it phonetically, out loud, softly, "Laxami, Laxami."

She smiled, dropping her eyes from his again.

"Why did your parents give you that name?"

"I don't know, perhaps they thought that I would bring them good luck, perhaps in memory of the twelfth and lost tribe of Israel." Standing she collected her bag, preparing to walk ahead of him, before she continued, "I never did find out. Perhaps I will see you on-board and thank you for the coffee." Turning, without waiting for his reply, she moved towards the exit, following the direction of the older couple.

Retrieving his coat Ethan quickened his stride to remain at an observable distance behind her. Through the boarding process and inside the aircraft, Laxmi disappeared around the forward galley-wall, drawn in conversation by two cabin attendants towards the crew quarters.

Ethan propped two pillows behind his lower back and relaxed, taking-in the tarmac activity as the aircraft taxied, bumped its way rhythmically to its takeoff position. He visualized the frame of the fuselage hesitate, for a divided second, locked behind the forward motion of the wings before it was picked up and dragged forward as the engines accelerated, straining to breathe on either side of him as the pilot committed the aircraft to their takeoff. The airport gave way beneath him, the river, surrounded by green, the city in the distance. He wondered when he would see it all again. He thought of Samara, realizing that he had no image of her in his mind. Soon, perhaps.

Beads of rain held tenuously to the outer window, forgotten momentarily, isolated from the slipstream of the aircraft as it climbed rapidly. Mitriann, he remembered her words, leading the emotions that she reinforced to him in her eyes. He replayed their evening again, what he said, what he did not say. Words and phrases came to him that had not entered his consciousness when they were together. What he could have said, what he should have said. Not enough time or was it that he had avoided other truths? He felt depressed, a closing of emotion within himself.

'I didn't talk to her about her feelings, about Samera. I should have taken our discussion further? She was open to it! Why not? Why didn't? Next time, when I return!'

Lost in a moment of self-criticism and disappointment he closed his eyes until another voice distracted his melancholy.

"You seem so serious, Ethan Judd, so intense. I am worried about you and perhaps I have just the remedy!" Laxmi offered a split of champagne and two glasses and sat beside him. She smiled, silent for a moment, inviting him to share his time with her. "I am curious, the older couple at the airport, the pleasure that you took in watching them, do you like that sort of attention?"

"Yes," he smiled comfortable.

"And do you have someone to give you that attention?"

The question drew images from an unfeeling distance in his mind; the figure of his ex-wife, imposed behind, between the image of Mitriann. Mitriann, a faded image but the essence of his regrets after all of these years. Counter emotion to his ex-wife, but a love that he knew, in his heart, that time and circumstance had distanced from him forever.

"No, I don't" he lamented, "and please call me Ethan. And you, Laxmi, do you have someone to fuss over you?"
She shook her head, holding his gaze suggestively." No, but maybe!"
Moving all of his doubts from the previous night to the side, Ethan responded.

"You know that I am taken with you!"

"Are you," she smiled, "why are you, why do you feel such a thing?"

"Sometimes there is a feeling that comes between people, once in one million meetings . . . do you know what I mean? This is one of those feeling for me. My eyes are enriched and," he smiled, raising his eyebrows, "let's begin with a toast to our possibilities. We can fuss over each other!"

"Well, a lot can happen between here and Paris, Mr. Judd," she said, "but we shall see."

CHAPTER IX

PARIS

Ethan fell-in behind Laxmi as she walked towards the automated exit doors of the customs area that provided a momentary blink of raw clouds and fresh air as they stretched, opening and closing, chopping, regulating the line of passengers in front of them.

He took-in her shoulders, her hair, styled by two tortoise combs, long, black, hiding the width of her waist. Laxmi, sensing his attention turned and smiled, encouraging him with nothing more than a parting of her lips. His response was a rush of excitement that he could feel in his throat.

They were unspoken in the taxi, each absorbed in their individual expectations and the visual distractions of the outer suburbs of Paris as they passed through and over them. Laxmi sat forward in the seat, a hand resting, relaxed on his knee. Ethan exaggerated the lean of his torso towards her, excused by the swaying of the taxi as it challenged the sharp boulevard turns. He listened to the rhythmical slapping of the window wipers, unseen sounds, stimulating thoughts of motion. He reached out to touch the fabric of her skirt.

Acknowledging his gesture, Laxmi shifted her hand to his knee as their taxi moved through the early Parisian winter weather.

Ethan's mind responded with excitement to the gesture. He was open to accept and enjoy her attention as it unfolded. His body relaxed to the motion of the taxi. He was open to the attention.

Unprompted, Laxmi placed the fare on the front seat of the taxi before they stopped. Ethan thought that they had driven the street once before, from the opposite direction but dismissed the idea, distracted by the blurring of the rain and the constricted stiffness between his legs. He leaned into her as he reached inside of his jacket for his wallet.

"No, no, it is done," she said, with a nod, a gentle frown above her eyebrows.

Retrieving her bags he followed as she moved ahead of him towards an unlit doorway, key in hand. He registered the rain reflected cobblestone street, compacted to a single lane by the dominos of automobiles and motorcycles on either side. The sidewalk was a study of activity.

Arabic cafes and Yiddish delis, a Vietnamese mini-market. Mloukhia, couscous. A working class arrondissement. He would enjoy experiencing the sights and sounds. Waiters serving sweet pastries and coffee to the men, veiled women completing their routines of shopping for the evening meal. Hanging chickens, bric a l'oeuf, dried herbs and fresh vegetables.

Laxmi glanced at him standing next to her in the doorway, bags in hand, waiting for her to open the double set of locks on the outer door.

Inside, she visibly relaxed, dropping her handbag and raincoat to the floor, kicking off her shoes. Standing to one side she snapped her head forward, her hair cascading downward as she removed the combs and brushed out the hair spray with a moan of pleasure. Ethan stood under the awning, bags in hand, not wanting to appear presumptuous, waiting for instructions.

"So what am I doing here with a man who I have known for less than half a day?" she frowned as if perplexed.

"Perhaps we have known each other longer than that!" he responded in kind.

She studied him before she spoke. "Do you have commitments for your time here in Paris?"

"Yes, some."

"What about tonight, are you free for dinner?"

Ethan shrugged, "No, I cannot tonight, I have some calls to make back to the States. But I'm free tomorrow night, what about you?" He hoped that a conflict of schedules would not cancel out their obvious interest in each other. He continued as Laxmi took the bags from him. "How long are you in the city for?"

"I'm hoping for at least five days here. I am waiting for a new roster, I have bid for Paris –Tel Aviv. I should get it because of my seniority, but you never know! And yes, I would like to have dinner tomorrow night with you."

"Great, say eight o'clock? You recommend the restaurant; I have no idea of what's here."

"I have a better idea; I will cook for you, here. I have had enough hotel food for the last two weeks and I am dying for a big salad and a relaxing time. I would like to cook for us. What do you say?"

Great, then I will see you tomorrow night. I'm at the Hotel Pont Royal in case something comes up. I hope not, but..!" He let the sentence fade as he retreated to the waiting taxi. He waved through the rear window to the figure that stood watching from the open doorway.

CHAPTER X

"Just a minute. Coming," Ethan heard her voice from the other side of the door before she open it wide to him. "Hello you beautiful man," she said, her arms outstretched "I have dinner almost ready for us."

Ethan touched his cheek to hers.

"And you too are beautiful" he replied, moving his lips towards her ear.

Half-heartedly, she shuddered in response. "Be careful," she smiled, "I have no resistance to that."

Encouraged, he moved his head deliberately, brushing her ear with his mouth, constricting her body gently within the strength of his arms.

She drew herself to him with a groan of approval and then, with equal strength, pushed herself away.

"Enough!" she protested with a deferring smile. "Leave me, make yourself at home in the front room. I don't have everything that I need for the dinner, I ran out of some things. I have to go downstairs. If you distract me any further we will go hungry."

Ethan smiled and moved into what visualized as a combination bedroom and artist studio. There were few female touches to the room.

"This is not your place!" he stated in a not so rhetorical manner.

"No, it belongs to a friend of mine. He is an artist, and no," she said walking towards him with a bottle of wine and a corkscrew, "he is not my lover, but he is away for a week and the place is mine until he returns!"

Smiling in recognition of the transparency of his question, he took the bottle with one hand and brushed his cheek against hers for a second time. She did not pull back as he kissed her gently on each of her eyelids and in kind to his gentleness, offered her mouth and her tongue for a moment.

"And now, while you open the wine, I must shop for our dessert," she said, leaning her head backwards, focusing her attention to his face. "There is a telephone if you want to make any calls."

"Actually, I might." He took the corkscrew from her hand and held her wrist, brushing her palm against his cheek as she pulled away and disappeared into the hallway. He did not follow but waited until he heard the outer door close behind her.

Sitting on the bed, he pushed his shoes neatly under the oversized oval window, as he placed a call.

"Operator, a credit card call to New York City, please." He paced the windowed wall, taking in the street below as the activity of the night unfolded.

"Gulf States Resources."

"Mr. Tony Booth, please."

The telephone was answered almost immediately.

"Tony, this is Ethan Judd. Yeah, fine. Look, I have reservation for you at the Pont Royal. It's in my name." He kept his voice light. "Yes, the Pont Royal. It's located on Rue Monte Lambert; it's named after the bridge. You should enjoy it and besides, it's confirmed on my credit card and there is no point in wasting money." He paused, listening to the sounds that bounced back to him from the other end of the line. "No, no, everything is fine. I'm a little ahead of our agreed schedule. I'll meet you the day after tomorrow, as planned. Yes, at the hotel." He waited, listening. "No,

Moscow was uneventful." He did not mention Prague.

His mind wondered laterally to Laxmi. How would he end the relationship that had such promise in its beginning? Reversing himself, he changed his questioning. It was their relationship to end, not his. He glanced at the wool-blanketed bed. This was her place. It was always easier to leave than to be the one left behind. Or was it? He thought of Laxmi's reaction to their moment of parting. Dismissing the thought he finished the call abruptly.

CHAPTER XI

Relaxed in their intimacy, Ethan kicked the top sheet away from the bottom of the bed and stretched his feet, crossed at the ankles, into the morning light that streamed from the window, pooling itself around Laxmi's clothes that had fallen the night before, abandoned on the bleached wood floor.

He reached for the smoking cigarette that Laxmi offered and rolled onto his back, his right arm resting on the pillow behind his head. He stared at the copper ceiling panels, following the contours of the ornate motive, registering the flagellant leaves of peeling paint. Laxmi watched him as the cigarette smoke curled inward on itself, upward, captured within the chilled sunlight. She waited for him to speak.

"To ask me if I loved my ex-wife is to ask me if I love being forty-four!" he said, the finality of his statement punctuated by a smile around the corners of his eyes as he chose his words in the exhaling of his breath. He did not look at her.

"I used to view my life like a sort of mosaic from afar, where all the patterns of my experiences since my marriage were woven together in an almost impersonal way!" Pursing his lips, he frowned. "Then, it got to be where I would judge her, take every interaction with her apart. But it was not really her that I was judging, it was me." He looked down at his hands, at the tip of his cigarette before he continued.

"Time is no longer a measurement. Losing time does not seem

critical anymore. Only today is important. The successes and the failures, actions never taken, desires set-aside, instincts ignored; and now, the mosaic has begun to take on a whole different image of its own. From a distance it looked strong, vibrant, confident, but up close, the edges are beginning to fray. He held up four fingers-full of his hair and smiled, "The threads are fading to white and the patches are wearing thin."

Leaning into her, supporting his head with her shoulder, staring at the wall, he read his unwritten lines without fore-thought or ego, frowning as if in pain. "To ask me if I loved her is to ask me if, at forty-four, her statement that, 'when we made love, she could hardly feel me' upset me, or if it was a statement of fact! It was unanswered bruises on her thighs; jealous hours spent waiting for her return from afternoon sojourns. It was soft telephone conversations that ended abruptly when I entered the room."

Turning, he held the depth of Laxmi's eyes to him. "To be forty-four was to have her either dressed and smelling of the garden, or dressed to exit when I came home but not to be dressed for me."

Covering his lower lip, he sighed. "It is to imagine revisiting with old loves, lost feelings. So many years. Emotions suppressed or diverted. What do you say? What do you do?"

He stopped, and closed his eyes. Samera was on his lips. Unable, unwilling to expose his vulnerability further, he held his breath, fighting to control the openness that he felt as a sadness filled his heart. His isolation dominated the silence in the room.

Laxmi moved towards him on the bed and reached to his face as he touched her palm to his lips, her unspoken gesture commanding him to lie back on the pillow. Sliding on top of him she held his face in both of her hands and kissed him with a gentleness that his heart embraced.

Responding to her touch he allowed his tears to fall, fulfilling a need until he felt the moment pass.

He wanted to challenge her, physically, to wrestle with her on the confines of the bed. The thought was exciting. To circle her, to grapple and wrestle with her; and equally exciting he could see it in her eyes as she seemed to read his thoughts, the challenging belief that she could keep him at bay and even master him. He wanted to rub the roughness of his whiskers against the back of her shoulders, to grasp her, to pin her between his legs, to have her surrender to him.

"Be careful!" she said, smiling.

He was physically excited. His nerves pulsated in his throat. Leaning forward, he stubbed his cigarette in the ashtray and turned, sitting on her lap, pinned her body within his arms.

"You be careful" he said. "I'm getting an urge to bite you!"

Groaning with inviting pleasure, she offered her ear to his advance.

"Mm, you can do whatever you want to me," she whispered, reaching between his legs, stroking him gently. "Within certain limits," were her last words before she offered him her mouth.

"You will have to tell me those limits," he smiled, moving her downward onto the pillow.

CHAPTER XII

Ethan opened the door for her and took Laxmi's arm as they descended onto the sidewalk. He sensed an excitement in the morning air. He was in Paris, arm in arm with a woman whom he had exposed his intimate self. No hesitation. No judgment. He was confident in their beginning and now he only wanted to enjoy her company and her presence.

They walked towards the river and his hotel; their conversation calmed by the closeness of their physical bodies, the contact of their eyes and fingers to each other. The city stirred to Sunday morning around them.

He was enjoying himself; he could not remember the last time that he had been this relaxed. He wanted to buy everything she looked at in the storefront windows, to shower her with gifts. How else could he express himself to her? This was so different than any of the trips when his ex-wife had accompanied him. The sex was as uninhibited, probably because of the absence of children and the hotel atmosphere he conceded, but he did not remember the sheer excitement of her presence as he did with Laxmi. He reached and drew Laxmi tightly to him and she responded in kind with a quiet murmur of emotion.

"I want to remember this moment," he said. "I am enjoying being with you, here, in the middle of the street, in the middle of Paris, holding you close to me." He moved his head away, taking in the colors reflecting in her hair. "I would like, I feel, a want to be with you, to spend more time together." He shrugged to express himself. "I'm not sure what it is, but it is something that I feel."

"You are a strong man, Ethan." She smiled, cuddling closer into the embrace of his arms.

He rocked her gently from side to side as she tilted her pelvis towards him.

"What do you mean," he smiled.

"You are so open in your heart to love and emotion, and that is unusual. It is something that I admire in a man."

"Are you making comparison to the other men in your life?" he asked, holding her rigidly, knowing that their embrace would be broken at any moment by the appearance of a vehicle moving towards them on the street, demanding egress around them, but a tinge of jealousy stimulated him, and he waited for her answer.

"No, there is no comparison, but you surprise me," she stated matter-of-factly.

Her openness stirred him; he wanted to know more of her.

"And you are a beautiful lover," she smiled, as if reading his thoughts. "Not the biggest, but size is not everything."

"Come on," he said, choosing not to lead with an obvious question, pressing her waist with his hands, "I want you off the street before we are run over and I lose you."

Laxmi took his arm, allowing him to guide her again toward the river and the Hotel.

The Pont Royal, close to Notre-Dame and the Louvre, dominated the narrow street between the Seine and the Boulevard St. Germain. The street was pressed to contain the motorcycles and an ambulance whose flashing red lights were constricted in a circular motion upon the stone frontages of the adjacent buildings. The commotion commanded the lovers, from a distance, to slow their approach. They watched the milling crowd huddling in expectation of a surprise appearance from the hotel entrance.

Laxmi reacted first. He could feel the firmness of her intent as she turned, steering him into the closest shop front.

"Wait here," she commanded, turning to the proprietor, asking for the usc of his telephone.

Behind chintz draped curtains of the store window Ethan watched the scene unfold at the entrance of the hotel as Laxmi followed the proprietor into the backroom.

The crowd separated in a singular backward motion and then slid forward, pressed to surround, to close a feeling of intimacy with the covered stretcher that appeared through the hotel entrance. Laxmi returned and took him by his wrists as she watched the stretcher being loaded into the ambulance.

She began quietly, excluding the proprietor in their conversation.

"Your friend is dead. We must return to the apartment. A car will come for us. You must hide."

Squinting in surprise, he acknowledged her statements with a question.

"Why, how do you know?" he asked, pulling his wrists free, moving his gaze back towards the window. "First Moscow, then Prague and now here! What is going on?" He turned back to her; the tension in his raised shoulder punctured the space around him, adding urgency to his question. "How do you know that Booth is dead?"

Laxmi bit the inside of her lip in anxious response to his question. She moved her eyes back and forth across his face before she attempted a response.

The shadow of a vehicle, a taxi, pulling up in front of the shop, its 'OCCUPEE' indicator illuminated, its headlights on full, broke the silence between them.

"Quickly," she pleaded with a sideways movement of her head towards the taxi, avoiding his question, grasping his coat sleeve in a gesture of urgency. "We must go. I will tell you all, later, but we must go!"

Silent for a moment, he followed her out of the shop.

Crowding behind her, they moved towards the taxi, its door open, inviting them, until a voice from a distance, jolted him to stop.

"Mr. Judd, Mr. Judd!"

He saw the man, moving toward the taxi, pushing, wrestling to free himself from the crowd surrounding the entrance way of the hotel.

"Judd, wait-up."

Breaking free of the crowd, looking quickly sideways in both directions, the man began to run towards the taxi, the breeze ballooning open his windbreaker exposing, for a moment, a glint of flat metal and leather that Ethan recognized as 'non-standard issue.' Laxmi saw it as well.

"Into the car, now," she urged, pushing him unceremoniously onto the back seat, throwing herself in behind him. The taxi lurched from the curb, its rear tires squealing in protest to the throttle pressure and the one hundred-and-eighty degree turn, before it retreated and then merged into the oncoming traffic of the boulevard.

"That was an American!" Ethan yelled in protest, separating himself from under Laxmi, looking through the back window at the diminishing figure standing in the middle of the boulevard, oblivious to the disruption of traffic that was accumulating around him.

Ethan grasped her arms demandingly toward him. "I want to know what is going on, now!"

"Wait," was all she said defiantly, turning away from him, her eyes making contact in the rear-view mirror with those of the driver. "Wait until the apartment."

They sat silently, the stillness compounding their tension as the taxi halted in the shadow between the streetlights. On an unspoken command from the driver, Laxmi opened the door.

Ethan's senses were on the edge of an adrenaline rush. "No control!" was all he could think of as he moved in her shadow towards the doorway of the courtyard. Laxmi turned the key quickly and pushed the door open as if for added urgency with her shoulder. Upstairs, they stood, hidden in the unlit room, at opposite ends of the bay window, silently, watching the cobbled street approach to the building. He could feel her as they both searched hungrily for odd movement in the shadows or a lack of it in the passing shoppers. The wavering trees, disbursed between the light poles, disrupted his view but he saw nothing.

Turning towards her as she exhaled audibly, deeply, releasing the tension that she held in her lungs, Ethan's eyes locked in recognition of the moment.

"Not yet," she pleaded. "I must talk with someone first. Wait until I return. Please, wait!"

He nodded once, his jaw tightening in unspoken frustration as she moved sideways, away from the window and disappeared downstairs. She reappeared directly below him on the street. He watched her fleeting figure, her hair sweep sideways, pushed by a gust of wind as she crossed the crowded street and vanished under the awning of the Algerian cafe opposite the building. He waited, unmoved, unsure of what he expected to happen next.

His thoughts raced, "Moscow, it started in Moscow! What the hell did I do in Moscow?" His eyes lingered on the center of the colored awning below that had engulfed Laxmi. "No dissidents, nothing unusual at the Trade Show. The Petroleum Ministry visit for Booth was okay." He moved his attention to the bottom of the cafe awning, looking for Laxmi's figure to reappear. He replayed the dinner meeting in his mind; the courteous exchange of letters at the Moscow Ministry. Nothing.

"Shit!" The words reinforced his own surprise as he backed away from the window and dropped heavily onto the couch. His heart pounded in recognition of his dilemma. "The exchange, what the hell did that guy give me?"

He forced his mind to recall the event of Moscow and Prague.

"Nothing," he thought. "Nothing. No problems with the authorities . . . " and then it dawned on him. The eyes of the little guy on the escalator. "The little guy who fell on me!"

Swinging to his feet, hesitating, remembering his agreement not to leave the apartment, he walked towards the doorway and followed Laxmi's exit, out of the building. He needed to find a public telephone.

"Mr. Booth's office. May I help you?"

He recognized the voice of Booth's secretary.

"Mr. Booth please. This is Ethan Judd calling."

"One moment please, Mr. Judd."

Out of change, he fretted that his allotted time on the telephone would run out before he was connected.

"Mr. Judd, this is Steven Rogers speaking. Mr. Booth is not in his office at the moment, is there something that I can help you with."

He could feel hesitancy in the voice and reacted abruptly out of frustration.

"I know he's not in the god damned office today. He's dead. If you don't know that already! Listen to me very closely, Mr. Rogers. I want to talk to Mr. Gordeon. You tell him that I will call back in exactly two hours and if he does not take my call the world will know of his deal with the Iranians."

The voice in New York was confused.

"I don't under . . . "

"You don't have to understand anything. You just have to pass the message. And you also tell him to pull off his man or the same threat applies. Have you got that?"

"Yes, but . . . "

Disconnecting the phone, glancing sideward at his reflection in the shop window as if for reassurance of his reality, he retreated back towards the anonymity of the flat.

CHAPTER Xlll

The door gave way, silently. The matchbook that he had jammed it closed with fell to the floor, the only discernible sound. Kneeling to retrieve it, Ethan waited, listening. The silence acknowledged Laxmi's continued absence. His ears screamed for recognizable sound, but they could not hear the shadow that appeared behind him as he moved into the light of the front room.

A Russian, the voice was Russian.

"Mr. Judd. You will come with me please. Without questions and without hesitation or I will shoot you where you stand."

Ethan raised his hands slowly and turned, his thoughts scrambled between his predicament and Laxmi. "Where was she?" He thought of her lying dead, someplace out of his sight, or still not here. "Fuck!" he thought, "Fuck!"

He measured the distance to the tip of the silencer that stared at him he. Discounting the possibility he tried to relax his body. He needed time to think.

"You are from Moscow?"

The statement took his intruder by surprise.

"No discussion, Mr. Judd," the man recovered, gesturing minimally with the base of his revolver towards the floor. "Sit down, please."

The man moved around to the window behind him and glanced

outside. He prodded Ethan in the back with his revolver while pulling one of the drapes closed. "Stand up, move, please," He picked Ethan's overcoat up from the couch and covered the gun.

Hands held above his elbows Ethan moved towards the door, his thoughts alert to Laxmi. "Where the hell was she? What could he do if she appeared in the doorway?"

He hesitated, controlling the urge to run as he saw two men appear from the rear doors of the Citroen that rolled quietly to a stop in front of the doorway, its idle engine creating a steady stream of rising vapour from its exhaust pipe. The pressure of the gun barrel in the small of his back commanded Ethan forward.

"Put your hands down and walk to the car, to the back door and get in. You were a soldier once, Mr. Judd, but more importantly, you are a family man. As am I. You have two children, I have one daughter and one yet unborn. You will know the hopelessness of your position. It would be my regret, but understand that I will kill you if you resist."

Ethan thought of his children. He thought of Samera. "Three children, I have three children." Lowering his arms he moved towards the car without protest. Guided into the back seat by the gun barrel jammed hard into his kidney his physical pain was overwhelmed by the frustration of knowing his fate was out of his control. Samera and Amie, Samera and Ashley, they would never meet!

He was locked between the two men, there was no escape. He looked out of the windows for a face of recognition as the door was pulled shut; there was no one. The driver took his cue and moved the car immediately away from the curb, jerking into the center of the narrow street.

"Sit back, Mr. Judd and look straight ahead." Ethan ignored the command and turned his head towards the back window in a last desperate hope.

He heard but did not see the clash of metal and front window glass, the momentary darkened blur of shoulders and arms moving through the air in front of the car. His head snapped forward, pulled by the momentum of the car as the driver, clenching the steering wheel, slamming on the brakes, thrusting his passengers forward. The driver began yelling in defense of his driving. The Russian reacted immediately.

"Shut up, you fool!" he yelled, opening his front passenger door, holstering his gun in one coordinated motion.

There was not time. A crowd gathered quickly. They surrounded the car, pinning it to the scene of the incident. In Gallic fashion they demonstrated the plight of the elderly woman lying face down on the street and her tangled bicycle on the hood of the car, one handlebar contorted, protruding through the shattered windshield.

The Russian moved into the crowd, towards the woman, and was lost quickly in the undulation.

Ethan struggled to disentangle himself from his jailers. He felt the raw air invade the car as both of the back doors opened simultaneously. He saw the blur of movement, he heard the unobtrusive spit of the silencers, he saw the feathered evidence of tranquillizer darts as one and then the other of his guards jolted forward again but this time without protest. In slow motion he saw a clenched fist, the butt of a gun move over him, towards the front seat. A dart in the back of the driver's neck cut short the beginnings of the man's movement for his own weapon. Manhandled by the scruff of his jacket collar Ethan was yanked towards the door of the car.

"Quickly, come with us!"

Stumbling over the body, he fell out of the vehicle onto the street.

Collecting him by his arms the young abductees began to drag him away from the automobile before he could get his feet under him.

"Stop! Stop or I will shoot!"

Ethan heard the order. He felt his arms freed as his rescuers turned to face the direction of the voice and he dropped instinctively to the ground as the gunshots rang out.

The Russian had moved out of the cover of the crowd and was shooting as he advanced deliberately towards them. One of the young rescuers changed weapons. The Russian, protesting his failure, staggered backwards against the car. A single bullet in his right leg shorted him from the confrontation but not before he saw the boy to Ethan's right, no more than twenty, crumple, like for like, bending silently to the cobblestones, his gun clattering as it bounced, announcing its neutrality.

The crowd scattered, hunched in panic at the outburst of the confrontation. The quiet that followed, five still bodies and one bicycle qualified the evidence of the dream. The crumpled figure of the elderly bicyclist was nowhere to be seen. Ethan raised himself from the cobblestones in time to be coupled again with his remaining rescuer.

"Move, now, before the Police come!" were the instructions and this time he did, without hesitation, running neck and neck, towards the alley connecting them with the distant boulevard. They were moving too fast to stop as a car, a back door swinging open, loomed in front of them, blocking the alley, their only means of forward escape. Ethan recognized Laxmi's face as they approached at full sprint.

"Into the car, into the car!" she yelled through the front window as the two men hit the trunk to halt their forward motion.

Tumbling, onto the back seat, they lay entangled, lungs heaving, demanding oxygen. Squealing tires grasping for traction drew little attention to the car as it reversed its motion. The back door slammed shut, bouncing off a stand of garbage bins holding their position at the entrance to the alley. Reversing onto the boulevard, the car melted into the afternoon traffic. Ethan, leaning his shoulders, the back of his head against the seat, his breath labored, turned to Laxmi.

She glanced at him over the front seat, her fingers to her lips.

"Wait," she said, "wait," as she turned her attention to the traffic in front of them.

CHAPTER XIV

"Laxmi!"

Forcing a smile, she moved towards him, leaning against the wall, her hands resting behind her.

"You startled me!"

Shrugging his shoulders, Ethan reached out for her.

"And you me!"

"We will be safe here, at least for a while," she said. "We will bring your bags." She slipped away from his arms, searching his eyes. "Are you all right?"

"Yeah, I'm fine." But he knew that the emotion, the intimacy of their relationship had, at least for the moment, dissipated.

Laxmi stepped forward and reached out for his hands.

"Don't say anything," she said. "Just hold me."

Quietly, holding her hands loosely, Ethan followed the screen of sunlight as it cast an inviting robe of brightness through the open doorway, onto the bed. He felt the physical restlessness that she aroused in him as he moved his arms around her shoulders, a little closer. For the longest moment he rested his cheek in the softness of her hair. He closed his eyes, absorbing her.

Laxmi spoke without disturbing their intimacy.

"You are involved in something I believe you are unaware of."

Ethan did not move. He waited for her to continue. "You are a courier," she stated softly, her hands holding gently to his waist, her eyes now addressing his. "And because of that, you are in danger."

His mind raced back to Moscow, ahead of her words. He reached for her hand and he led her, out of the bedroom, towards the source of the sunlight. They sat on the edge of the overstuffed couch, knees and thighs touching, trying to hold onto something, no matter how tenuous.

"What is it that I am supposed to be carrying?" he asked.

"Documents, a micro-film of documents."

"Do these documents belong to you?"

Laxmi lowered her head until it touched his shoulder in gentle intimacy.

"No," she said, leaning against him, "I work for Israeli Intelligence."

The honesty of her gesture was not lost to him.

"The Massad!" he stated rhetorically.

"Yes."

"What are these documents?" he asked, "Were they passed to me by the Iranian?"

He saw a brief flicker in her eyes. She did not know about the Iranians. He waited.

"No, by someone else. We believe the documents are meant for delivery to your current employer," she shrugged, "It could be as simple as that. But we are not sure!"

Ethan studied the colors overflowing from her hair, his mind replaying his encounter on the escalator in Moscow.

"I don't understand!"

Her voice was tired. "I don't know the details, but we believe that the Moscow courier was compromised after the micro-film was deposited with you. It is, or was, to be delivered to your employer."

"Here in Paris?" he asked quietly.

"We think so."

Looking down at her hands, he turned towards her.

"And my hotel rooms, in Moscow and Prague?"

"No," she said, her brow furrowed, "We do not know who that was. Not yet anyway. It took us a day to trace you after you changed your schedule. Someone was ahead of us. We suspect Russian Internal Security."

"Jesus!" he exclaimed, his eyes narrowing in surprise. "And the Pont Royal?"

Turning, she laid her hands on his wrists.

"It was not us, Ethan. We are unsure of what happened. We think that your friend might have interrupted someone searching your room."

"Someone looking for the micro-film! Who?" he asked, thinking of Booth and his moment of death. He was beginning to feel numb. He had not felt an adrenaline rush like this since he lost his first platoon sergeant in Vietnam.

"Yes," she nodded, "and now we believe that the French Surriete must be putting the pieces together through Interpol and," with a gesture of her hands, "we believe with your CIA!"

"The American at the Hotel, the man with the gun?" he questioned her again.

"Maybe," she shrugged, "but we are unsure."

Rising, he stood in front of her. "What do you mean, 'unsure?' Aren't you working with the French or CIA on this?"

Dropping backwards on the couch she invited him to step toward her. She sighed in response.

"No! Since Putin things have become confusing in many ways for us. But in this case, it seems that all sides are after you for their own self interests."

She spoke again as he turned away from her, toward the window. "As for the American, he may have been free-lance."

"Free-lance! Who is free-lance?" He turned on her, trying to control his frustration.

"The American may have been working for your employer, or he may have been CIA, or he may have been working for someone else, a third party. We don't know yet," she said, pausing between statements for emphasis.

"What does that mean?" he asked, dropping next to her again.

Laying open the palms of her hands to him, she responded quickly, "Just that we are checking everything, but for the moment, you are not safe, you must hide."

He studied Laxmi's eyes, her cheeks surrounded by the softness of her hair as the sunlight highlighted it in front of him. He pressed his lips to the cathedral of his fingertips.

"What is it that I have?"

Realizing how much she cared for him, Laxmi could not hold to his line of questioning. She took-in his sweptback hair, curling around his ears and his collar as she reached out to him.

"Ethan, please speak to me . . . "

"Not yet, Laxmi. Answer my question first."

"Industrial drawings, mathematical formulas, engineering calculations," she said, her eyes never moving from his face, "that's all I know." Her voice was open in its honesty, her need to show her trust in him.

"So they are not military documents?"

"No, they are technical drawings of a nuclear power supply that could, will, change the balance of power in the world forever. It is the answer to five hundred dollars a barrel oil and the need for the US and China and Europe to continue to carve out their global oil and gas sources with invasion and 'keep out' signs.

"What is the technology, Laxmi?"

Laxmi shrugged. "I do not know the details, only what I have picked up in passing. It uses radioactive nuclear waste as its source material. No fission, no fusion." She dropped her voice, "The formula was stolen by a Jewish émigré, the brother of one of the Russian scientists working on the project in Moscow. It was top secret. We did not know about the project, we know very little of the technology and, we did not we know of the plans to steal it. We only became aware of it only after one of the émigré group was arrested by Russian Internal Security. We think that he may have been the courier who was to pass the drawing to you.

"I have told you, I know nothing about this, Laxmi."

Laxmi shrugged and continued, "I believe you, Ethan. But because of that arrest, Russian Internal Security unbeknowingly got too close to one of our Moscow intelligence cells. Otherwise, who knows!" she smiled, "the technology may have ended up with your employer and the thieves may have already retired to a warmer climate than Moscow as wealthy men, if that was their intent."

Ethan slipped off the sofa. He looked quietly out of the window, his left thumb brushing his lower lip.

"So." He raised his eyebrows as he turned to address her, using his fingers to define his calculations. "So, the thieves want it back, or at least want to make certain that I deliver it to complete their deal with my employer, whose man in Paris is now dead.. The Russians want it back. I take it that your people would like to have it or you wouldn't be here!" Laxmi did not react to his statement but waited for him to continue. "The French will be in the hunt if they aren't already and the American interests, my employer and or the government, or others have already shown their hand!" He allowed the slightest of a smile to appear as he continued, "And the assumption is, that I have it and know about it and am on the run!" For the first time in a while he felt some semblance of control again. At least now he knew what was going on and what he was facing, if not the who or the size of his problem. The decisions were his and he would make them.

Laxmi did not return his smile. She was still, her eyes steady, imparting a message of their own.

"All I know at the moment Ethan is that men have already died for these secrets and I can assure you that your life and probably that of anyone else who gets in the way is expendable without a moment's hesitation. These are stakes of power and influence that the world has not experienced since the Chinese began their move into Africa for their oil and mineral needs."

Feeling her mood Ethan fell silent. He watched her, recognizing his own needs, unspoken. He turned his gaze to the floor, unwilling to lead the conversation as he asked a single question.

"What is our relationship, Laxmi? Was it ever real?"

She reached out for his hand as if to ease the tension between them.

"You must decide, Ethan. I am open to you, but you must decide."

He did not move away, but turned towards her, again.

"What do you want from me? What are you expected to do? Retrieve the documents or do I also become expendable?"

Clasping his hand with the outer tips of her fingers she focused all of her attention to the question.

"You must decide."

Drawn to the limits of his defenses Ethan sighed, knowing how good she made him feel and yet afraid to let go. Sensing his dilemma, Laxmi leaned toward him and reached out with her free hand.

"All I know is that I want to be with you. All I know is that I want to love you. The rest can wait for a moment in time. I have no other answer for you"

Ethan closed his eyes, not wanting to reply, not wanting to question or challenge her motive. He felt her closeness, could smell her body as she reached out, her palms open, reaching for his touch.

"No, Laxmi, no! It is too early for this. I need to think."

CHAPTER XV

A knocking on the outer door, urgent, disruptive, drove itself between their tensions. Laxmi moved silently to the door. Ethan did not move, his quiet belying the tension that he felt.

He could not discern her conversation, conducted through the confessional of the unopened door. He waited, conscious of the sunbeam, the quiet of the room, listening to the movement of her feet as she retreated from the hall. Her eyes told him that they were not going to pick up where they had left off.

"The Surriete are only minutes away," she said, balancing to put on her shoes. "We must leave immediately."

Ethan followed her out of the apartment and onto the stairwell, upwards, without question. His ears absorbed the sound of commotion and protesting voices below them. Hesitating, he followed her glance downward through the stairwell to the depth of the foyer before she resumed her pace with a terse command.

"Up, quickly."

Three flights of stairs opened onto a garrote landing. Laxmi moved to the only door. It opened easily to her pressure. Ethan brushed past her into the darkness and waited as she closed and locked it behind them.

He followed her outline, his eyes straining to adjust to the looming shadows in the storage-room as they groped towards the only source of light. Ignoring the darkened masses that fell away from him, he followed her shortened command.

"The skylight, quickly."

Sliding a chest-of-drawers into the stream of light, he raised himself up and pounded on the swollen wooden frame of the skylight with the palms of his hands, his knees bent, re-enforcing the effort of his blows.

Laxmi watched the urgency of his exertion, alternating her attention between the movement of his hands and the direction of the door that separated them from the staccato of climbing footsteps.

Struggling, pounding, a slither of light from between the broken dry-rotted cross ribs encouraging his efforts. Prying loose one side of the distorted box-frame, he jiggled it until the whole frame sprang upward, muffled by the static of protest pounding on the opposite side of the defending door. Raising his arms through the opening he jumped, catching the outer frame with his winged elbows and, kicking in front of him, pulled his body up, through the small opening and onto the sloping tiled roof.

His presence disappeared for the briefest of moments before, catching hold of the frame again, Ethan thrust his head and shoulders back in the cavity, his hands constraining his lunging body. His eyes strained again to separate the light and shadow in the space below him as he called urgently.

"Laxmi, get on the dresser, take my hand."

He could not see her. He could hear her moving away from him towards the door but he could not see her. He heard the door handle chattering in empty motion and male voices, high pitched, protesting angrily to the resistance of the lock as they pounding with buttress shoulders to break through.

"Ethan, go! Go now! If you need help, go to 16 Rue du Tobac. It is in the nineteenth arrondissement, ask for Madam Simone. Use my name.

16 Rue du Tobac. She will help you."

He strained to find the figure lost in the darkness below until the sound of wood, splintering around the door lock, forced his decision. Raising his body quickly out of the opening he dropped the skylight frame back into place and stamping it shut for an added head-start.

Turning to the ridgeline of the rooftop he reconnoitered his only escape route. He took a deep breath and stutter-stepped along the steep pitch of the roof, arms outstretched for balance. Precariously, at the mid-point of the roof, he grasped for the growth of television antenna that sprouted from between the tiles, willing that they would not give way to his weight.

He hated heights. He hated ladders as a boy. He hated parachutes in the army, and he hated the idea of falling seven stories off a moss covered Paris rooftop.

Wiping the perspiration from his eyes, he drew the courage in his lungs to go on. He did not look back as he heard the skylight bouncing, springing open again behind him.

One square chimney obstacle away he could see the iron rungs of a fire escape leading downward. How far downward he did not know, but it was a means of continuing evasion from his pursuers.. With a single breath he disentangled himself from the contorted metal reeds that bowed and waived in protest toot his roughness. Stealing a quick glance in the direction of the male figure emerging from the skylight, he launched himself, arms extended, feet straddling the worn roof caps for balance, towards the chimney. The urgency of an unseen voice behind him, demanding him to halt, struck him as funny.

"Keep going, don't look down, don't look down." His lungs screamed openly, venting his adrenalin, releasing a brood of pigeons from somewhere close, unseen, that distracted his last faltering steps. The leather of his shoes chaffed against his anklebones as he contorted them sideways along the roofline.

Flailing forward onto the buttress of the chimney, eyes closed, ripped fingernails confirmed that he was safe. Bear-hugging the chimney, he sat, preparing to drop the four feet to the flat roof below.

Hidden from view, he could hear the shuffle of his pursuers as they began to trace his path across the pitched roof. From the silence he knew that they were as hesitant as he had been.

Dropping quickly off the buttress, his body bent forward to avoid the hanging lines of clothes washing, Ethan ran towards the iron ladder. The metalwork dropped landing-by-landing below him, until, by his best guess, it fell away between the first and second floor.

"My luck to break a leg," was his first protest about the distance.

Still hidden from sight of his pursuers he retraced his steps to the roof doorway, pushing it open. A diversion to encourage investigation. Racing back to the ladder he glanced down to re-confirm its path to the street below. Pulling himself up and over the rampart, he descended quickly, hesitating only on the first floor landing to muster his courage before dropping towards the pavement. He rolled as his feet hit the sidewalk.

The last that his silent pursuers saw, from their high vantage point next to the chimney, was a figure disappearing into the rush hour traffic as it turned the boulevard corner without looking back.

At the subway turnstile, loose pocket change determined his furthest destination.

CHAPTER XVI

Silently, singularly, Ethan emerged from the subway station. The arrondissement, another working-class neighborhood.

He drew his coat collar drawn high and with hands hidden in his pockets moved quickly towards the plastic neon announcing the welcome warmth of the closest café and the anonymity of people.

The cafe held the heat of bodies, steaming the windows, deflecting the glances of passers-by, warming him from the chill of lost energy as he stepped inside. He moved to a table in the rear of the cafe, close to the kitchen exit. He ignored his neighbors and they did him. His coat, patched with dirt, shoes scuffed from his escapade, his pants showing water marks, and his hands dried blood, discouraged curiosity.

Seated, facing the door, he allowed himself to relax. The first cigarette made him dizzy, displacing the oxygen that had supported his flight. Outwardly, he seemed to be daydreaming, lost to an inner turmoil as he tried to make sense of his circumstance and evaluated his options, his courses of action as they came to mind.

Searching for coins in his pockets he moved towards the peeling 'TELEPHON' sign painted on the men's room wall.

He listened to the call ring of the telephone. No time to think. What if Samera answered? 'Hi, this is your father! I would like to talk but the time is not good. My life is in danger and I need your mother's help. Is she at home?' Or Janos, 'Look, I understand why you didn't come to dinner the other night and I would like to talk with you, but not now, and by the way, is your wife at home?' 'Christ, let it be Mitriann who answers!'

"Mitriann? It's Ethan!" he said, his head bent to his chest, arresting the relief in his voice. "Yes, I'm in Paris, but listen, I'm in trouble. I need your help." He shifted the weight of his feet in response to her voice. "No, it has nothing to do with Samera, it's something that I must work out, but I need somewhere to stay for a couple of days, and I'm going to need some help. You and Janos are the only people I could think to call!"

He balanced the phone against the crook of his neck and waited, listening to her muffled dialog with someone at the other end of the line. Janos!

"Ethan," she said calmly, the reception springing crystal clear, can you tell me more? What have.. how serious is.."

Ethan cut her off in mid-sentence, and addressed what he knew would have been Janos's questions. 'Mitriann, I have not done anything illegal, at least not knowingly. I seem to have gotten myself involved in some sort of industrial espionage I don't want to use my credit cards and I am running out of cash. I just need somewhere to stay for a few days to work things out." He waited for the statement to be passed on.

"Ethan, my cousin, Stefano Greganos, the son of my father's brother. Go to him."

Ethan repeated the address as he reached into the toilet stall and unraveled a wad of paper, dipping it in the running water of the sink, washing the dried blood from his fingers as he thanked Mitriann and hung up the phone. Splashing water on his face and rubbing his hands dry on his coat he moved back to the table and ordered a double cognac for his coffee. He asked for coins for another telephone call.

Forced to wait outside the men's room he lit another cigarette and shuffled his feet to announce his presence to the back of the figure occupying the telephone. He didn't look up, unwilling to engage in any contact with the patrons who moved obliviously past him to the pissoure. He moved quickly to the handset as the telephone came free. The odor of garlic reeked from the receiver as he placed his call, to Florida. He pumped the telephone box with coins.

The concern in his ex-father-in-law's voice through his disorientation of being awakened from what Ethan knew would have been a heavy nap was obvious.

"Ethan, are you alright? Where are you? Christine called, there have been two calls for you at home, she's anxious to get-- hold of you. The Russian embassy called, something about your visa . . . "

"Granddad, listen to me," he said, jumping on the echo as calmly as he could, "I'm okay, but I want you to take Christine to Jo Anne's cabin. Have her take Amie out of school and fly down there first thing tomorrow. Can you go and stay with her?" He did not wait for a response. "I'm in Paris and I'm in a bit of trouble. I don't think that there is any trouble for Christine or for Amie but I don't want to risk anything." He could hear the older man's hesitancy.

"Okay, I'm sure that we can use the cabin. Jo Anne's down in Miami so it shouldn't be a problem. Umm, I know that it's your business, but can you tell me what's going on?"

He tried to make light of the question.

"Oh, it's a complicated story, Granddad, but I'm okay. I just don't want Christine involved. Tell her that I'll repay her for the tickets."

"Oh, okay! Where are you now, Ethan?"

He wanted to cut the conversation off without causing alarm.

"Paris, Granddad. Look, I'll call in a couple of days, okay?"

The statement gave some confidence to the conversation.

"Oh, okay. I'll call, uhm, what time is it now, anyway?

"Four in the afternoon, your time."

"What time is it for you?"

"Almost midnight."

"Okay, Ethan, I'll call Christine right now. Can you tell me . . . "

He tried not to show his impatience.

"Okay, thanks, Granddad . . . and tell her not to tell anyone where she is going, okay?" he added, almost as an afterthought.

"Okay. I'll tell her that you will call in a couple of days. Take care of yourself, okay!"

"Yeah, okay, bye, Granddad."

He cut the line dead without waiting for a reply and lit another cigarette before heading for the rear of the cafe and the subway.

CHAPTER XVII

The door was opened by a child, no more than ten. The unraveling shoulder seam on a jersey was all that Ethan could discern through the crack in the doorway and the safety chains that separated them.

He questioned the sleepy brown eyes that studied him suspiciously. "Esker Monsieur Greganos esse s'il vous plait?" The door closed quietly before he finished his inquiry. He waited, the silence prodding his anxiety. About to knock again he heard the dismantling of the chains that isolated him in the hallway.

The woman glanced towards the stairwell before she whispered to him, "Que esk que?"

"Je suis Ethan Judd, Madame," he nodded his head up and down in assurance to the woman. She pinched his coat sleeve and gently pulled him inside the pensione with a conscious, deliberate look down the murky hallway, the light bulbs long removed from the ceramic sockets for their cash value. The sound of the door chains sliding back into place invoked an inner sigh of relief, recognition that, at least for the moment, he was safe.

The room was warm in its colors, the aroma of saffron and lamb. Heavy rugs absorbed the sound of movement and the light colors of the divan blossomed from the constriction of the room.

With a gesture of her hand the woman invited him to sit, before she disappeared through the beaded curtain into what he assumed was the kitchen. She did not return. Not feeling that it was his place to follow her he waited until, finally, unable to forestall the tiredness of his body, he closed his eyes in rest. He was asleep long before the child moved into the room and sat opposite him, watched intently, without moving for the longest time.

Ethan woke to the demands of his bladder and the sound of whispering voices. The muscles in the back of his neck were stiff as he lifted his chin slowly off his chest and raised his protesting eyelids. He was not alone.

A man was surrounded by matching sets of brown eyes, all connected to his arms and legs by the touch of a hand, the resting of an elbow, a head, a knee or a bottom.

"These are five of my children, and I am Greganos" the man began with a gesture of his hand, exposing the expansive bulk of his figure as he leaned forward.

Ethan's smile to the ensemble was not returned as they were introduced to him, one by one. Each possessed something of their father; the deep set eyes, the Roman nose, the heavy, dark hair, the broad bone structure that stretched taunt the smooth olive skin. Only the bushy moustache was not represented in its expansiveness.

"And I am Greganos," he repeated, gesturing to his barrel chest, smiling broadly.

The children took the lead from their father and also relaxed. The girls tempted each other to giggles and the boys smiled through full lips and teeth, one like the other.

"You are a lucky man to have such strong sons and three such beautiful daughters," Ethan volunteered with a smile to each of the children.

Greganos scolded the girls with a smile as they hid their mouths, silencing their impulse to giggle as he nodded to his guest.

"To my friends I am Staveros. I do not know if you remember, we meet at my cousin's wedding, many years ago in Hungary!"

"No, but I vaguely remember the moustache! Although there were a lot of moustaches if I recollect correctly"

Staveros leaned forward in his armchair, laughing as he dismissed his children with his physical movement.

"Good, now that formalities are finished, you will tell me why my cousin has asked me to protect you in this wicked city!" he smiled, finishing his sentence with an introduction of his wife who interrupted them with a tray of sweet tea. 'You must be very special for my cousin to ask for your protection after so many years!"

Ethan shrugged his shoulders without responding. What was he going to say?

Staveros moved on when the silence told him this was an area not be questioned. "When did you eat last?" he asked, gesturing with his head towards Ethan's coat, "and for how long have you been on the streets?"

Taking the tray from his wife Staveros dismissed her with a smile before Ethan could thank her for the tea. "Bring him some food, Mother."

Raising himself heavily from his chair, untangling his weight from younger arms and torsos that reattached themselves to his body and with tray in hand, he led his guest into the kitchen. "You eat and then we will talk." He dismissed the children one by one with kisses and waited for Ethan to begin.

"Actually I've only been aware that I have been in trouble for the past ten hours or so." Ethan volunteered, rubbing the back of a crooked thumb over his chin. Staveros raised his eyebrows in surprise at the statement.

"How I got like this is another story but, in a nutshell, I am in trouble and I do not know who I can trust. First though, I have not, to the best of my knowledge, done anything illegal. I would not involve Mitriann or any of her family in that." Lifting a spoon, he continued. "There have been three kidnap attempts, one I think by Russians, one by Israelis and one by another group."

"Kidnapping! Of who, of you? Staveros injected.

With a mouthful of breakfast stew and baguette, Ethan hesitated for a moment, before he continued, "And a mistaken identity has resulted in the death of a business acquaintance."

Staveros stirred the sugar lumps in his tea, unspoken, waiting.

Ethan counted with his fingers. "My hotel rooms in Moscow, and Prague, and now here in Paris, where my business acquaintance was murdered, were all burglarized. Somewhere there is an unknown American looking for me and, judging from the speed in which I was found this afternoon, I think that the Surete must be involved." He leaned forward, depositing the spoon in his bowl. "One of the problems, Staveros, is that I don't think that any of them are working together, at least to the best of my knowledge." His silence announced that he had finished speaking.

Staveros lit another cigarette and frowned over the left side of his forehead as he absently scanning the plastic table covering and the small electrical stove.

"If you say that you have done nothing wrong, then what do they want?" he asked, the smoke pacing the contortion of his lips and tongue.

"Industrial drawings."

"Do you have these drawings?"

Ethan leaned backwards, formulating his thoughts. The sound of guitar chords from the next room allowed him to deflect an immediate response to the question.

"Moreya," he said, listening, leading with his eyes towards the cords of music in the next room.

Staveros smiled in proud recognition. "My son. You surprise me, perhaps my cousin taught you more than she told me!"

Ethan took the statement no further.

"What happened in Moscow that has caused you all of this trouble?" Staveros queried, rocking back and forth, balanced on the back legs of his chair. "How did you end up with these drawings? And if you know what the Russians want, why not just give it back to them?"

Ethan concentrated on his answer, "One, because I haven't figured out what and where the drawings are, and two, there has already been one attempt on my life. My problem is that I don't know who it was and, therefore, I don't know how to deal myself out of the problem!"

'If you don't know where the drawings are, how do you know that you have them at all?"

Ethan was reluctant to implicate Laxmi by name and worked around the question.

"Perhaps it might be better if there were things that you do not know, Staveros, for your own safety sake!"

"No, no," Staveros responded quietly with a pendulum movement of the cigarette held between his fingers, pointed at Ethan, "you cannot come into my house and put all of us at risk and not tell me everything. This is not what the request from my cousin asked me to do. Tell me all or tell me nothing and leave as quietly as you arrived."

There was silence between them for a moment.

"Okay," Ethan responded, "look, I'm sorry, no insult intended."

"And none taken, my friend. Besides, I do not know what I can or cannot, or will or won't do for you, yet!"

Ethan began again. "I was told by someone in the Israeli Intelligence Service, a woman who saved my life earlier today, that I am the courier of these drawings and that my life is in danger."

"Was this for her own purpose? To make you reliant on her?"

Ethan shook his head in the negative. "No, at least I am almost sure, no."

"So if we assume that the Russians still want you alive in order to retrieve their property, who wants you dead? Who killed your friend" Staveros frowned, "but then again, it may not have been the Russians. It was not you who was killed!"

Ethan warmed to the "we," an acknowledgment that he had an ally.

"Staveros, what I need is time; I need time to figure out who is after me. I need names and faces. To make a deal.

"Or to get yourself killed, Ethan."

"Maybe, Ethan shrugged, 'but right now I need time to figure out who I can trust and who these people represent!" Reaching for a cigarette, he continued, "The drawings are on micro-film, I think I know where I came into their possession in Moscow, and I think I know where they are now. But I will need your help! My clothes and my bag, you must get them for me. They are, or at least they were, at the pensione that the Israelis took me to after the kidnapping attempt. Incidentally, three men were put out of commission during my rescue. They were immobilized with tranquilizer darts but, another, a Russian, was shot and wounded.

Staveros exaggerated his cringe as he performed the sign of the cross. "Of, Mother of God, Ethan, do not tell me all of these things."

Acknowledging the brevity, Ethan continued. "The Surete may

still be there, but maybe not. There may be danger!"

Staveros crossed himself again, "Not a problem."

"Mmm, one problem," Ethan exclaimed, moving quickly to his feet, pacing the restriction of the kitchen, "I don't know the address."

Staveros waited for him to continue.

"Okay, okay, I know how to get to it." For the first time in three days Ethan felt some control. "Go to 16 Rue du Tobac and ask for Madam Simone. Tell her that I sent you but, in order to verify her identity, ask her for the address of the safe house that I escaped from. That is where my bag is."

Staveros smiled. "Again you surprise me, Ethan, are you sure you don't have a little Gypsy in you?"

Ethan returned the smile of this stranger whom he was beginning to like.

"I will send my oldest boys, they can move in the streets better than me," Staveros stated, his smile as wide as the sparkle of the rings on his hands. Rubbing his stomach he moved towards the living area. "I am too handsome not to be noticed and, besides, who will remember two ragged Gypsy boys?"

The guitar music stopped as his host disappeared from the kitchen. Ethan pushed the plate aside, too agitated to finish the food. He finishing his wine in one breath before Staveros returned.

"It is done. Arturo and Polys will leave in a little while. They will watch the street tonight." Staveros spoke with his hands, protective of his sons, "tomorrow morning, when I say it is okay, Arturo will visit with your Madam Simone." "Now," he said with a smile, fanning his fingers in front of his nose, "you sleep, but first, you take a bath!"

Ethan awoke to the smell of coffee and fried bread.

Stepping through the kitchen entryway, he slid his fingers through his unruly hair. "Bonjour," his embarrassment at being the last one to awaken disappeared as the children made a place for him at the table and the fried bread and coffee were set before him. Staveros and his two sons were absent.

Ethan lit his first cigarette of the day only after the children left and decided to shave before the day unfolded further..

Staveros was waiting for him as he appeared from the bathroom.

"You were taken to Rue du Phillip de Brois. Number 46. My boys are on their way there now to retrieve your belongings. They will bring them, if they are still there!" Leading the way to the kitchen Staveros continued, "We must wait for their return."

Ethan followed behind him. "Did the woman say anything else?"

"She wanted to know if you were safe. The boys said 'yes,' and told her that you would contact her when you were ready!"

Pouring coffee from the stove, Ethan offered Staveros a mug. He was feeling better.

"Good! The boys must not return there in case they are recognized."

"Ethan," Staveros interrupted solemnly, "You forget that they are Gypsy men in a foreign country. We know what to do!"

Ethan lowered his cup as he spoke.

"Staveros, I am sorry. I am a guest in your house. You have put yourself and your family at risk for me, and my life is entrusted to you." Shrugging his shoulders, he continued, "I . . . "

Staveros stopped him with an upraised palm. "Enough, we understand each other, my friend."

Ethan measured the time by the stretching motion of the shadows beyond the windows of the pensione. His anxiety was distracted only when the boys returned with his clothes and bag in hand.

They dropped the items noisily, like trophies, in the middle of the floor. Ethan waited while they spoke excitedly, proudly to their father who stood in front of them, arms outstretched, his wrists resting on their outer shoulders. Roaring with laughter, Staveros kissed each of them on the right cheek and sent them to the kitchen where Ethan could hear their mother fussing over them. Chuckling, Staveros addressed his guest.

"There was a gendarme on duty but, it seems, a mysterious newspaper fire in the hallway one floor below your safe flat distracted him long enough for the boys to find your belongings!"

Ethan moved into the kitchen, his smile was as broad as Staveros's as he ruffled the heads of the grinning boys before he shook their hands.

"Staveros, tell your boys," he said without taking his eyes from them, "that I am in their debt, they are my guardians."

"Not so serious," Staveros laughed, "they are already over-confident from the day's work. Rather tell them that they should be careful, I feel it will get more dangerous before we are finished."

The reality of the statement was not lost on Ethan as he moved back into the sitting room and sat cross-legged in the middle of the floor, confronting the mass that represented his belongings. Staveros, with some difficulty, joined him.

"What are we looking for?"

"I don't know exactly, a foreign object, anything that could carry a micro-film. It was put there in haste so it shouldn't be difficult to find." He passed his overcoat to Staveros to search before he began to methodically empty the shoulder bag, remembering how he had found it in Prague following the burglary.

"I left Moscow one day early than expected, four days, three nights ago, and since then my movements have been random.. Not by design, but that's the only reason I'm one step ahead of whoever it is that's after me!" Shifting his attention to the individual contents of the shoulder bag, Ethan continued, "I'm sure it was Russian State Security who tried to kidnap me yesterday, I mean, I know that they were Russian. That much I do know. At the Hotel, an American came after me, I don't know if he was a government man or a private operator possibly working for my employer or for someone else, but he was armed!" Rubbing his temples with his fingers, he looked up at Staveros, "and now, the Surete are involved. That I know because they chased me over the rooftops. They could have shot me, but they did not and your son's have confirmed their presence at the safe house! The Israeli's thwarted the Russian kidnap attempt, but for what reason outside of their own interests, I do not know. I mean, maybe that is enough. The question is, who are my enemies and who can I trust?"

"First things first, my friend," Staveros said, ripping open a half empty pack of Marlboro cigarettes and examining the inner lining. "Your bargaining chip is the possession of these drawings. If your kidnappers yesterday were Russian State Security, and they knew where the plans were, as I said before, I do not think that you would be here with me today!"

"You're right," Ethan replied, rubbing his temples again with the palms of his hands as he did when he felt under pressure.

"Then let us keep looking for your salvation," Staveros continued, turning the pockets of the overcoat inside out.

Ethan turned his shoulder bag upside down in similar fashion, shaking it to confirm its emptiness.

"It's got to be small. I don't think that it would be in the lining of my coat or my clothes or the bag, no time, and to much chance for it to fall out or for me to throw it away unknowingly. It's got to be a foreign object."

They began their inspection again, in silence. They could hear the gas jets on the stove, boiling water their only distraction until the aroma of fresh brewed coffee called them to a halt.

Stretching his cramped legs, Ethan sighed. He could see nothing that was out or place or not his.

"Perhaps I have lost it, or thrown it away already! he shrugged.

"Perhaps," Staveros said, nodding in rhetorical agreement. "But let us pray not. Nobody else knows that, and so your risk has not changed!"

Switching positions silently on the floor, Staveros offered a cigarette. Ethan drew heavily on the tobacco.

"What is the same but is different?" He had been good at the game thirty years ago in Vietnam. The circumstances and the objects were different, but the logic of ambush was the same.

Roaming the objects in front of him, cigarette smoke rising from the cigarette between his fingers, he rocked forward on his crossed legs. Leaning on his left fist, he gently prodded a box of matches with his right index finger before he picked it up. Invited by the sound of sliding content, he opened the box.

"Bingo," he whispered.

Watching him, Staveros stopped his exploration.

"What is bingo?" he asked, waiting for Ethan to continue.

"Something familiar, something new!" he smiled. Reaching into the matchbox he removed a five-star Soviet red and white Young Pioneer pin and held it up to the light between his thumb and forefinger.

"What do you see?" Staveros asked.

Ethan was still smiling, "We swapped American-Russian

Friendship pins at the Trade Show in Moscow, but I don't remember putting anything in a matchbox and I do not remember collecting this, a Lenin Pin!"

CHAPTER XVIII

Ethan glanced at his watch waiting anxiously for someone to answer the phone. Midnight, eight o'clock in Washington. He jumped at the voice.

"Simon? Oh, Stuart! This is Ethan, is your dad at home?" He had never begun a conversation so abruptly with the boy but he was in no mood to discuss baseball cards and school band.

"Okay, would you get him for me please? I would like to talk with you, Stuart, but next time, okay?"

He timed Stuart senior's walk from the living room to the phone in the hall. Six seconds from his lazy-boy chair to the phone.

"Stuart, yeah, Hi, it's me. Look, I need some help!" He did not feel like regurgitating his predicament again but realized the necessity if he was to expect any immediate help.

They had been friends at Boston University together. Separated by distance they had drifted apart after he had volunteered for Vietnam, his friend avoiding the issue by staying in school, but they stayed in touch through the years, at least at Christmas.

"Stuart, I'm involved in something that I'm not sure about. If your people are not involved, then I'm sure that they would probably like to be or should be."

"Oh. Is this phone secure? Can you tell me what it is? You know that I'm only an Analyst, I'm not sure that . . . ?"

Stuart, as cautious as ever, always predictable. He ignored the questions.

"Yes, I know, Stuart, but I need to know if your people are involved and if they are, whose side I should be on! Someone tried to kidnap me yesterday and I don't know who's who. I don't know who to trust, Stuart. I need your help." He emphasized the word 'your.'

"Jeez, Ethan. I'm not sure what I can do, but sure." Stuart continued, his voice buoyed by the confidence expressed in him. "Where are you and how do I get a hold of you?"

"I'm in Paris; I'll call you about the same time tomorrow night."

"Oh, okay! Is there a number where I can reach you if something comes up?"

"No, I'm going to move around a bit. Tomorrow night, okay?"

"Sure. I just thought for emergency reasons, but okay, tomorrow night," Stuart repeated. "How's the family?"

"Why do you ask?" Ethan jumped.

"Jeez, Ethan! You are jumpy! Are things really that serious? It's just that I haven't spoken with you for a while. Amie must be ten by now!"

"Eleven." Judd relaxed his voice. 'Typical of Stuart to try and end their conversation on a pleasant note.'

"Stuart, I've got to go!"

"Okay, tomorrow night, Ethan, bye."

Ethan disconnected the line with a finger before gently replacing the phone back onto its hook and exited the phone booth.

CHAPTER XIX

Madam Simone made herself visible on the port railing of the tour boat, following Ethan's instructions. She gazed calmly at the rippled surface of the Rive Gauche parading past her, oblivious to the man playing catch in a circle of Gypsy children close to the tour dock. Her concentration was on the meeting that she expected to have, she was conscious only of her back-up leaning over the stern railing behind her.

The man on the bank did not recognize her, but saw another, standing on the deck above her, a red scarf in his hands, fluttering in the breeze created by the movement of the vessel. A pass.

The woman was not alone.

The circle of children continued to play until the double-decked boat disappeared under the Pont de la Concorde and followed the concrete perimeters of the Quaides Tuileries towards the Petit Palais.

Ethan returned to the pensione, frustrated, edgy that the woman had not followed his instructions.

From the look that Staveros gave him, he knew that word of his aborted meeting had already been received.

"Tonight you must leave this place. My brothers, Calva and Rabio, they will move you to a safe house. They will stay with you."

At the safe house, away from the innocence of children, there was no attempt to hide the weapons, the knives, keener than those required to slice the l'pomme de terre offered on the table.

CHAPTER XX

Ethan chose the cafe randomly to place the telephone call. The conversation would be short. He would be long gone before the call could be traced.

Stuart answered after the second ring.

"Ethan?" the voice volunteered.

"Yeah. Hi."

"Look, I don't have much to tell you, I need another day . . "

"I don't have another day, Stuart," he interrupted, aggravation evident in his voice. "What do you have?"

"Well, we don't know yet, but your activities have been recorded by the Embassies in Moscow and Prague. Something about a series of burglaries. But we do know that Russian Internal Security investigated the burglary in Moscow and that's unusual! Is this phone secure?" he asked, almost as an afterthought.

"It's as secure as I can make it. It's a public phone."

"Okay, okay. But we need another day. Will you call me tomorrow, same time, at my office?"

"Stuart!" Ethan drew out the name, "this is the first time in twelve years that you have volunteered your work number at the Agency!" He continued flatly, "Don't bullshit me, Stuart, what else do you have?"

"Nothing, Ethan, honestly. Something is going on, but we don't know what. We need a little more time!"

"Who is 'we,' Stuart?"

"Oh, I'm sorry, that's me and my Section Chief, Phillips."

Ethan fell silent. He could think of no immediate alternative.

"Six hours. That's all you've got. Give me a direct line. No transfers. No putting me on hold while they get you from the john!"

"Okay, six hours, I'll make . . . "

Ethan hung up the telephone before the statement was finished and retreated to the toilet, waiting for the shoes and white socks in the only stall to exit.

Emerging from the back of the cafe, Ethan lifted his collar against the chill and walked without hesitation, away from the direction of the safe house. Things were not going to plan. The timing was not good. He could not see the brothers but was comfortable, knowing that he was under their surveillance, close by. Calva behind him, Rabio somewhere on the other side, ahead of him.

Thirty minutes, two street reversals later, he was back in the warmth and security of the pensione. He waited twenty minutes for Staveros to appear.

"I have friends who will help us," was the man's only comment.

CHAPTER XXI

Ethan slouched in the back of the car, his face and torso hidden in the shadow of the door, hands in his pockets to help retain his body heat, his stillness belayed his presence to passersby. He was irritable. He had slept on the couch, in his clothes and now, seated in the car, nerves in his feet and back were beginning to aggravate him. He cringed his toes to compensate for the feeling, but he needed to move around, to stretch, to renew his pinched circulation. He wanted a shower, the flow of hot water on his neck and shoulders. Discipline said 'wait.' He wondered if the windows, fogged by the warmth of his breath, would alert an observant pedestrian. Who were they, who were they? But then again, it was not out of the ordinary for down-and-out Parisians to sleep in their cars, on and around their possessions. The locked doors and the revolver in his pocket gave him marginal comfort.

He watched, with idle attention to the detail of the line of transient men, forming, waiting for breakfast at what he assumed was a Soup Kitchen. He wondered where the women slept, where they went for a dose of gospel, coffee and starch.

"Limited meals, the early bird gets the voucher." Ethan watched those whose crutch was their physical ailments, the aged, for whom the Mission offered companionship, the down-and-out whose silent demons distracted them from a reality of loneliness, emptiness without love.

"Not hard to end up here," he thought, wondering where his

endeavors would lead him in twenty years, in two years, in two days. He thought of his girls, he thought of Samera, until the wails of an ill defined North African song interpreted on guitar, moving in a low-slung Citroen interrupted his self-indulgence.

He watched Calva emerged from the pissoure, running his hands through his hair, an all-clear signal. Scouting the shadows behind him, Ethan opened the backdoor and stepped out, his right hand holding firm to the revolver enveloped in his overcoat as he moved across the street to the public telephone booth reserved by Rabio's bulky presence. Ethan was anxious, he needed to calm himself for the call he was about to make.

The brothers moved into the shadows, away from the telephone booth, as he lifted the receiver.

"Eth..."

"Stuart, get Phillips for me," was his only communication.

"Ethan, I . . ."

He could visualize the two men at the other end of the phone line.

"Stuart, get Phillips for me. Last time . . . or I talk to either the French or the Israelis."

He did not know if he was bluffing or not, but then neither would Phillips.

"This is Phillips, Mr. Judd," the voice stated authoritarianly. "Please try to remain calm. It's in your best interests that you follow my instructions and . . ."

Ethan tried to visualize the man standing next to a nondescript metal desk in a nondescript office from the voice. Phillips wouldn't be his real name either.

"Phillips, let's try this once more," he said, raising the timbre of his voice. "Once more, or I'll interpret your response to mean that you are not interested in what I have in my possession and I am happy to talk to the French!"

"Alright, Mr. Judd, but listen very carefully. When you talked earlier with Stuart, we did not know what was going on!"

He could sense the concession in the man's voice as he began to backtrack his position.

"Is this a secure line?" the officiousness crept back.

"How in the fuck do I know how secure the public telephones are?" Ethan responded angrily. "All I know is that you've got three minutes to convince me that we're on the same side or I'm gone and your people will find an empty telephone booth."

Ethan glanced quickly around the empty sidewalk as he listened to the silence.

Phillip's voice deteriorating somewhere between a snarl and a whine. Ethan's confidence level grew two notches.

"Okay, Judd, don't be so melodramatic."

"Two minutes and forty-eight seconds. Your ego is crowding your time, Phillips."

"Fuck you, Judd . . . "

"Two minutes and forty-five seconds."

"Okay, okay. Listen, I don't want to have to repeat this . . . "

"Two minutes and forty-two seconds."

"What do you want, Judd," the voice shrilled. "What the hell do you want?"

Ethan covered the mouth-piece as a couple skirted the telephone booth. He waited for them to pass. "All I want is the truth, Phillips, only the truth," he stated calmly.

He heard the deep expiration of air through the man's nostrils carried over the telephone line.

"When we talked this morning, I, we did not exactly know what was going on. We knew that you were involved in something but nobody knew what."

"And do you know now?"

"Well, I, we think so, we have pieced . . . "

"Who was the American?" Judd interrupted.

"Not one of ours," the voice stated definitively. "His name is Carson. Freelance. We think that his client is one of the Seven Sisters, one of the oil companies, or maybe more than one!"

"Yeah, that would make sense," Ethan stated, moving into the flow with the dialog, giving nothing away. "So I must assume that he is not friendly!"

"We think so," Phillips answered succinctly. "As best we can put it together, you have been one step ahead of Soviet Internal Security since Moscow." Phillips digressed, "that's very impressive, Mr. Judd, we would be interested to know how you were able to do that."

Ethan resisted the diversion. 'Keep going Mr. Phillips. Two minutes"

Phillips did not protest. "Right. Anyway there's some shadow group we haven't been able to identify as yet who is also tracing your whereabouts. Maybe a terrorist group of some sort, unknown affiliation, possibly a Red Guard splinter group."

"No, they aren't terrorists," Ethan volunteered. "Soviet Jews, émigrés. I think they trashed my room in Moscow."

"Well, émigrés or not, Judd, they're unpredictable!"

"They're not my friends, Phillips, that's for damned sure!" he snapped.

He took a deep breath, stamping his feet to keep his circulation moving. "Touchy," he thought, "slow down, you'll lose control of this."

"And Prague? The Hotel passed it off as a cat burglar. Too much of a coincidence! Who was it?"

"We don't know yet, but Soviet Security alerted their Czech counter-parts to find you. That's what got us curious about you. No details though!" Phillips continued, "Do you know the name Major Andre Cosarkov?"

"No," Ethan answered, leaning his head down towards the mouthpiece of the telephone.

"His name was on the communiqué," Phillips continued.

"Describe him."

"Soviet army regular, infantry, Afghanistan. Five-nine, sandy hair, left handed."

Ethan remembered the gun. "Yeah, I've met him. The Israelis took him out."

Phillips blustered, "What! We are not aware. . . ""Later, Phillips, keep to the story. Your three minutes are almost up."

The voice slowed with some relish, "Well, it seems that you are in deep shit, Judd. It appears that your escapade with Cosarkov got the Surete interested, and now they're looking for you as well! We don't think that they have the whole story yet. It seems that everyone wants you, but no one is asking for cooperation."

No, it says that no-one wants your cooperation, Phillips. It does not say that no-one else is not cooperating. You could be getting frozen out of this, you know!"

Phillips hesitated, thinking about the possibility. "Whatever, Judd. But it tells me that you are up to your ears in something." The voice continued sarcastically, "You're out of your league; otherwise you would not be calling for help!"

"Phillips, you have not asked me why everyone is after me which tells me you either know, or you are completely in the dark," Ethan responded calmly. "In the dark as to why the Russians tried to kidnap me, why the Surete are chasing me and some unknown group wants me dead. You don't know do you?

"Well, no," the man calling himself Phillips began, but I, we assumed that you are calling for help from your government, after all, why else would you be calling and why else would I be taking my time on the phone with you!"

'Phillips, you don't have clue. Resonant Nuclear Technology. Ask your friends about it and when they tell you that it is in the realm of the mad scientist, you can tell them, 'well actually no, the technology has been proven by the Russians. And when they ask you how you know this, you can tell them you have been speaking with someone who has the only complete set of technical drawing for the commercialization of the technology."

"Judd, I don't know of this technology."

'No reason you should until now. But ask your scientific people."

Phillips voice was subdued on the other end of the phone. 'I don't know this technology or its value. I don't think that anyone will have an interest in nuclear for quite a few years now, after Fukushima Dai-ichi. But obviously you think that you are on to something. Give me a couple of hours to make some calls myself and I will call you back."

"No, I will give you one hour and I will call you back at this number" Ethan was firm as he hung up the phone.

The hour passed quickly. Another arrondissement, another café, another public telephone. Phillips answered the phone on the first ring.

"Judd, I've spoken with some people who would be very interested in talking with you about the technology. "

Ethan heard the emphasis on the word 'very.'

"Phillips, I have a microfilm, I"

"Yes, that's all very well, but our friends will want to examine the contents before we…"

Ethan was angry. "Phillips, what don't you understand? Is it your arrogance or your disbelief that this technology could be created outside of the States? If you don't get aboard with me on this I will go elsewhere to make a deal."

"Judd, just a minute," Phillips protested, "are you talking with anyone else about this?"

"Or," Ethan continued, "I could copy all of the interested parties, except for Carson, and you of course, and then you can explain to your bosses and they can explain to the American people why the biggest thing to happen since the splitting of the atom is in the hands of everyone except the US. The answer to end the US involvement in every misadventure in the Middle East and Africa, the end to dependence on oil." He continued before Phillips could interrupt. "Or, I could consider bringing it to you!"

"Well, that would be the most reasonable avenue," the voice began encouragingly.

"Or, I could sell it to the highest bidder," Ethan added matter-of-factly.

Phillips was taken back.

"Sell it! How can you put a value on something that you don't know about?"

"Well, neither do you, Phillips, but I think that you are getting the picture!" Ethan released his words softly, emphasizing the 'it.' "The Russians want it, the Israelis want it, the French and some Russian émigré group want it, and," his voice raising in exclamation as his single breath began to run out, "the Seven Sisters want it although perhaps not for the same reason as the others, and someone in that group, and that category might include the American government, has decided that if they can't have it then I'm duck soup!"

Shifting his stance, he felt the pain in his knees from the previous night's rooftop retreat.

"Someone tried to take me out yesterday, Phillips, and let's just say that it adds value for me." He waited for the man to reply.

"What do you want, Judd?" the voice asked coldly. "Do you want out, do you want our help? Just what the fuck do you want?"

"Three minutes! " Ethan responded, "your time is up. I'll call you tomorrow, same time, and Phillips, have an exit plan ready for me if I need it and a price for the technology" Removing the phone from his ear, he disconnected the line.

The brothers took their cue. Drifting out of the shadows they joined him as he retraced his steps across the puddled cobblestones towards the automobile. Ethan spoke without looking at either of them, hands in his pockets to hide their tremble as his adrenaline began to let down from the telephone call.

"I want a meeting with Madame Simone tomorrow. A safe place and I need the best photo processor that you know. You will arrange if for me?"

Calva fell into lockstep beside him and grunted in acknowledgment.

Reconnoitering the street in both directions as they reached the car, Ethan opened the front passenger door and melded silently into the seat.

CHAPTER XXll

The open faced brick grotto ceiling held the smoke filled haze that was only momentarily diluted each time the heavy wooden door was opened to allow entry or exit to recognized patrons.

Ethan entered behind the brothers. Holding the handrail he squinted, absorbing the high glare of the light that dissipated over the tables as they descended into the noise and presence of bodies.

Eyes at the tables acknowledged the Greganos brothers, ignoring him, as they moved in single file towards a table made ready for them. Ethan took his cue from their silence as Ratcina and four glasses were clinked onto the table.

He forced his attention to the far wall, ignoring the movement of people around him as they in turn reciprocated the gesture. Three solid drinks later he wanted to remove his coat. He was flush from the liquor but decided against the inference of relaxing in alien surroundings. The three men leaned into the table, silent, their posture discouraging visitors. The brothers acknowledged an occasional greeting with a slight nod but no one spoke, no one interrupted their isolation until Staveros, appearing from behind the bar, moved towards them, stopping, talking with those who called his name or moved to him in greeting. The brothers visibly relax as they watched their older brother approach the table. No one stood.

"Speak," was Staveros' only word as he sat and leaned into the table, pouring himself wine, topping off the other three glasses.

Ethan leaned towards him, the volume of his voice tempered by the distance between them.

"I don't know," he said, his eyes holding those of Staveros, his shot glass held above the table between his straightened palms. "The Americans wouldn't answer me. I really don't think that they know what is going on. At least not at the level that I am talking with. I hung up on them. You know what happened with the Israelis this afternoon."

"You do not trust your own?" Staveros asked quietly, holding Ethan's eyes with his.

Lighting a cigarette, Ethan left the pack on the table for the others. The gesture was ignored. They waited for him to answer.

"No, I don't," he stated firmly. "I saw too much hypocrisy in Viet Nam and today, it's a different stage called Iraq and Afghanistan and Wall Street greed and bailouts, but my Government is a government of the few for the few. I'm not naive enough to think that any goodwill gesture to them on my part will do anything except get me killed!" He fell silent. The brothers looked to Staveros to continue the conversation.

"That is bad. I have been told that the Surete have orders to double their efforts to find you." Raising his eyebrows, Staveros continued, "You are a very popular man, my friend. But, for some reason, I do not think that the French are working with the Americans to find you. What you have must be of great interest!"

"No, I agree. I do not think that anyone is cooperating with anyone. And yes, what I have is now safe, Staveros, but the question is 'how do I get myself out of this mess!'"

Standing, Staveros pushed the chair back with his legs. "That is your question, my friend, and it must be your answer. We will help you where and when we can, but now, we must leave before you attract anymore unwanted attention. We are safe here, but you cannot stay, we must hide you again. "

Foretelling the future, as Ethan reached for his cigarettes, the foursome were distracted by an outburst of confrontation, of commotion at the top of the stairs. A protest, a warning to those below. The doorman, buttressed from behind by another, was obstructing the determined advances of three gendarmes, distinguished by their blue capes and peaked hats and one other who moved behind them.

Staveros was the first to react. He moved quickly and the others followed, absorbed into a group of men congregated at the bar. In isolation Staveros slipped behind its wooden expanse and down, into an opening in the floor that invited their retreat.

Ethan stayed close behind Staveros as they descended, one-by-one, in a bobbing stream of motion, into a pungent darkness of spilled wine and the stale dampness of the cellar.

Reaching out with his left arm and grabbed the loose coattail of Staveros' leather jacket as he stumbled behind him in the moving shadows projected downwards from the single stream of light flowing through the open trap door. Calva and Rabio descended behind him.

Staveros struck a match above his head, illuminating his face as the cellar door closed silently above them. He held a finger to his lips.

Darkness to light to darkness. Staveros struck another match, lighting a kerosene lamp retrieved from the stack of wine cases beside him. Adjusting the smoking wick and, unseen to the others, he released another trapdoor that gaped uninvitingly within the dark wooden flooring. Blackness, a swirl of mist. Rabio moved forward, crowding Ethan, watching the lower half of Staveros's leather jacket disappear into the void, beckoned by the darting illumination of the lamp held in front of him.

Ethan grasped the edge of the floor planks for support and followed the glow from the lamp that distorted the uneven cobblestones behind and between Staveros' legs. They were in the sewers beneath the city and again he gave himself over to Staveros.

Struggling not to lag, Ethan slipped along the edge of the walkway, ripping his pant knees and his skin. Moisture exuded from the walls in concentrations of moss and slime, neutralizing his ability to balance with his hand before it puddled on the catwalk, building enough momentum to spill into the sewer culvert. The brothers helped him to his feet without protest as they stumbled over him. He labored to move in measured unison with his guide, conscious of the vapors snorting around Staveros' neck as he traversed ahead of him. His ears were alert to the crescendo of rushing water somewhere in the darkness in front of them.

Staveros slowed, offering, without turning, an unnecessary warning, as if to himself, "It is slippery here." By example, he grasped solidly at the guardrail of the small iron bridge that appeared along the catwalk, framing an overhang of emulsifying, glistening water that contorted almost silently from an aquifer deep in the brick wall, barging its way heavily into the foaming mass that stalked silently, restlessly parallel to them.

Ethan smiled to himself, accepting the warning with recognition of the aggravated pain in his knees as he prepared to follow, watching Staveros' foot placements.

Staveros did not slip. He stumbled forward and fell, clutching at his right leg as it jammed behind him, his muted cry of pain overwhelmed by the latent echo of a gunshot cascading through the unseen passages ahead and behind them. Ethan dropped instinctively, drawing his revolver as Staveros, pulled himself to one knee and dragged his leg another body length before he fell forward onto the puddled walkway. Rabio pushed Ethan aside and raced openly across the catwalk, revolver drawn, and began to drag his hobbled brother into the cavity of the closest aqueduct.

Ethan watched the figures, hesitant in the distance behind him, appear and fade through the rising, circulating mist before he fired, almost in unison with Calva who stood, shielding the retreating figures of his brothers.

Staveros called, unseen from behind the concave wall of the aquifer, "Calva, take him, you know what to do. We will give you time."

Calva turned to stay, hesitating, but for a moment, to protest the command.

"Go," Staveros yelled, sensing his brother's dilemma. His command echoed downward, absorbed into the waterway behind him.

Calva scrambled along the exposed catwalk and barked at Ethan to follow him as a pattern of gunfire and ricocheting brickwork chipped from the wall above his head, tracing behind his stumbling advance into the rush of water that challenged him.

Preparing to follow, Ethan fired two rounds into the dissipating mist that momentarily halted the advances of their nemeses.

"Go!" Staveros yelled again from behind the angular turn in the wall, exposing his face and an arm as he let off a single round, his revolver jumping in his hand. "Go, we will be alright." Retreating again behind the wall, he continued, "I don't know how they found us so quickly, something is wrong. Are they Surete?"

"I don't know," Ethan called, "they are too far, I can't tell."

"No matter, we will give you time," Staveros moved out of the shadow of the culvert opening again. "Go with Calva, he knows what to do. You must rely on him now. No one knows these tunnels like me, but he will take care of you." Punctuating his statement with another round of gunfire that passed en-route over Ethan's head in the direction of their slowly approaching stalkers, he continued, "I don't think that they will shoot you unless they have given up on whatever it is that you have."

"Comforting thought. We shall see." Ethan responded.

He heard Staveros laugh, "Are you sure it is safe, my friend?"

"Yes, Staveros, it is safe."

His words were smothered as Staveros fired again, starting him, on all fours towards the foaming water. Immersed, the cold surrounding sheared the raw nerve endings of his bloodied knees. Drawing to his feet, hidden from any angle of fire, Ethan waded towards Calva, the sound of Rabio's revolver covering his retreat. Calva urged him forward with a gesture of his revolvered hand. The water buffed high; to his crotch by the time he reached the waiting figure who nodded him forward with an upward thrust of his jaw.

Laboring, they traversed level by level the cascading field-width aquifer, fighting the strain of lungs and the relentless flow of choppy water for every foothold of forward motion. Calva approached the opening first. Hugging the wall, his senses urged caution to the exposure of his body. He signaled Ethan forward. Emerging side by side they began a slow, splashing shuffle forward through the ankle deep water, its presence hidden by an overhanging mist.

They moved into another set of chambers. Shadows lit by an overhead grid of lights. The sound of their heaving lungs and the splash of water bounded and tumbled against the walls within walls. The sound of tire traffic vibrated above their heads as Calva found an exit to the street above, its presence advertised by the iron ladder bars embedded in the wall. He did not hesitate.

Ethan crouched, his revolver drawn and cocked facing the direction of their retreat. Without a word Calva pocketed his gun and moved deliberately up the ladder. Straddling the top rung with his feet, he raised the manhole cover allowing a seam of light to sweep around him. He turned to orientate his direction and watched the on-coming traffic, moving over and around him. Ethan waited tensely for his instruction to move.

The surprise of rubber on metal, the front tire of a passing car slamming the grid cover down into its cradle, snapped Ethan instinctively deeper into his crouch as he looked upwards.

An inflamed "Merd!" was the only response from the dangling Calva, who, almost unbalanced from his perch, again raised the iron cover.

One, two cars, three cars, a bus, a motorcycle. They listened to the sounds above them before Calva made his move. Sliding the grid aside, pressing his body up and through the opening, he sat on the edge of the hole and swung his legs free. Casting a glance at the on-coming traffic, he yelled downward into the hole for Ethan to follow. Standing to his feet, facing the blare of horns and traffic from the on-coming traffic, Calva protected the gaping hole.

Ethan walked the rungs of the ladder upward to the street surface and emerged from the cavity. Replacing the lid, he turned towards Calva who stood, arguing with the driver of an automobile idling in front of the manhole, hostage to Calva's unyielding stance. A blur of blinding traffic blared their horns impatiently behind them, uneven lights and drafts streamed past them on either side from ill-defined vehicles.

Grasping Calva's arm, the two men turned and, dodging the on-coming traffic, traversed to the sidewalk of the boulevard before they disappeared quietly into the darkness.

CHAPTER XXIII

Cresting the path on the bicycle, Ethan recognized the second figure sitting on the open bench. Calva had signaled a party of two but he had not thought for a moment that it would be Laxmi.

Standing, pressing gently backward on the foot brake he allowed the bike to absorb the undulations of the path as he glided to a balanced stop in front of the bench. His eyes locked with those of Laxmi.

The older woman, watching him, turned to her younger companion and smiled.

"It seems that we have more here than you told me!"

Laxmi sat quietly, the meeting was not hers. Ethan, unwilling to concede a truth, looked away, forcing his attention to the other woman. Both women were motionless, demure, parallel figures. Madame Simon's hands rested neatly on her lap.

"Perhaps a signal," he thought.

He felt like a self-conscious teenager disguising his awkwardness by leaned on the handlebars, talking with a first real girlfriend. Laxmi raised her hand and covered the smile she could not contain. Acknowledging his predicament, Ethan smiled with her.

"Now, Mr. Judd, why have you sent for us a second time?" the older women asked.

The question drew his attention away from Laxmi, but the smile did not leave his mouth.

"Because you did not follow instructions the first time, Madam Simone. You were not alone then, as you are not alone now."

"A precaution, Mr. Judd. A precaution then and a precaution now."

Dismounting from the bike, Ethan set the stand before responding to the statement.

"Yes, but one that cost me two days, Madame, and almost cost me my life." He caught a movement in Laxmi's right eyebrow, but no other reaction.

"The aquifers!" the woman stated, the grey of her hair absorbing the light as the sun streamed through a roaming gap in the tumbling clouds.

"They were your people?" Ethan asked, the seriousness of his question manifesting itself in a deep frown.

"No, Mr. Judd, but you forget," she smiled, "our time with the Gypsies goes back much further than Auschwitz, especially the older generation."

He nodded without taking his eyes from her.

"Why did you send for me?" she asked, shifting the momentum.

Ethan lowered his head. She sat quietly, waiting for his response.

"Trust," he said, looking up at her. "The blood of my family is Jewish. Maybe I haven't come to an open acknowledgment of what that means." Gesturing, with his hands, palms up, he raised his eyebrows, "maybe there is something that says 'this is right!'"

"And your Mother, was your mother Jewish?"

"No., spent time in a Roman Catholic orphanage, I was told. I was raised by my Grandmothers, one Jewish and the other, not spiritual but a good and sympathetic woman he volunteered, his smile widening.

"So you are not Jewish, unless you define lineage as the Arabs do, by the father," she stated with a sideways smile at Laxmi.

Ethan nodded with her.

Madame Simone returned her attention to him. She studied his face, searching for an understanding of the man who stood before her. Laxmi watched them both, a schoolboy with a senior school mistress.

Ethan moistened his lips and prepared to speak, anticipated her next question. "That which was lost, was never lost. It is safe, for the moment."

The woman nodded in recognition of his statement.

"So speak to me, Mr. Judd. What do you want?"

He stepped towards her, not wanting to sound the beginning of an interrogation, answering the question with a question.

"What does this technology mean to you?"

Madame Simone looked at him, the truth of conviction evident in her eyes, her voice matter-of-fact.

"It means energy, it means self-sufficiency, an end to our total reliance on the pleasure and whim of the United States to support our requirements, perhaps our very existence."

Measuring time in a passing barge behind him, she shook her head and continued.

"We would not be able to keep the secret for long. I suppose that we would eventually have to offer it to the world!"

"With terms and condition?"

She nodded affirmatively and looked at him.

"With terms and conditions. Probably. I suppose. I do not speak for the policy makers of my Government."

She looked at Laxmi and then back to Ethan. "I have no illusions of today's world, Mr. Judd. Israel cannot afford to stumble, to fall behind, for who would help us to our feet but our own? The Jackal has followed us since Gethsemane. There is no reason to think that it will let us rest, that it will let us live in a contented peace for very long! We must extract a balance, an IOU, an obligation where and whenever we can."

The inference was not lost to Ethan.

"You do not think that the US government..."

The United States will only support Israel until Armageddon and the second coming of Christ, which they seem to be hastening Mr. Judd, or until the Middle East oil is gone and they do not need us as a counter-balance" Madame Simone hesitated, "and then we will be marginalized as the Arabs are today. Religion and oil, these are what drive the world today. Let us hope that the second coming is postponed for a little while longer."

Laxmi turned her face towards Ethan distracting the silence that followed the statement.

"What are you going to do?"

"I don't know," he said with a softening around the corners of his mouth, "I don't know yet."

He looked at her, time measured by the breeze that brushed past his face.

"What can we do to help?" she asked, returning his gaze.

Shifting his torso, facing her directly, he gestured with a furrow on his brow.

"I don't know yet," Ethan repeated, "but I need to know. I need to trust that it is not you who is trying to kill me! That will be a beginning."

"You have my word My Judd, it not us who are after you, Madame Simone stated emphatically, "Laxmi has told you truthfully of how we stumbled into your circumstance. Yes, we want the technology, but your death serves us no purpose. We are perhaps the only ones that you can rely on!"

Ethan turned to Laxmi, trying not to telegraph his feelings to Madame Simone's words.

"You were not hurt the other day? How did you get away?"

"I did not," Mitriann responded passively, shrugging her shoulders. "I hold a Diplomatic Passport, they could not hold me!"

Ethan bit the inside of his cheek, hesitant.

"These games, this intrigue, are they usual for you?"

Feeling the pain, the betrayal in his question, Laxmi stood and whispered quietly, "This one is not, Ethan, this one is not."

Reaching for her fingers, he pressed them into his hand.

"Then walk with me, now. Talk with me."

Closing her eyes, Laxmi exhaled deeply, squeezing his fingers in response.

"And you talk with me, Ethan, you talk with me."

CHAPTER XXIV

"The message is for Mr. Gordeon; please tell him that Mr. Judd sent me."

The stiffness of leather in Calva's coat sleeves sounded their newness as he folded them in front of him.

Recovering from the silent appearance and recognizing the finality of his statement, the Receptionist communicated his presence over a telephone, her eyes giving away the location of the voice behind the array of closed mahogany doors surrounding the oval foyer.

Calva turned to face the double doors, before they opened inward. He watched a man move towards him, adjusting his shirt cuffs under a hastily donned suit coat, its collar still turned up.

"I'm Jim Gordeon," the man stated as identification, extending his hand.

Calva ignored the gesture.

"You will bring the package and follow me, Mr. Gordeon. Mr. Judd is waiting for us. He is not a patient man these days."

A head shorter than Calva, Gordeon stepped forward, filling the distance between them, dropping his right arm.

"Does he have . . . "

"That is between you and him, Mr. Gordeon. I am to bring you to him. That is all I know."

Gordeon studied the face of the messenger.

"I was to bring one person with me, a company engineer, to validate the information that Mr. Judd will exchange with me, but I want to bring another as well, to protect my interests, you understand!"

Calva shrugged his shoulders.

"This will not be my decision. The risk is that Mr. Judd might not meet with you, but we shall see!"

Gordeon nodded, squinting, calculating his position, the twitch in his rigid eye betraying his nervousness. "Please, wait one moment," he asked, moving back into the office.

Calva could not distinguish the conversation that followed. Nor did he try.

Gordeon reappeared with another. An odd couple. Gordeon, in a three-piece suit, slicked silver gray hair, an oversized gold ring on his right pinkie finger that Calva assumed, from the raised lettering, identified him with something American; and his companion, a sweater jacket and a small undistinguished box, bound with string, held, as if an offering, with both hands.

"Mr. Tyrell, our engineer, his office is on the sixth floor, we will meet him there, if that's okay?" Gordeon volunteered, medicating his nervousness with words.

Ignoring both men, Calva recalled the elevator. The Receptionist, uncomfortable with the stiff silence of the three men, broke into a staccato of sound on the keyboard of her computer.

She watched them disappear into the elevator, in what seemed to her an unnatural order: the rough gypsy, Gordeon and the moody American, Carson.

Calva watched the floor indicator blink as it registered their descent. He turned toward Carson when the light illuminated the eighteen floor. Depressing the emergency stop button with the palm of his left hand, he gestured to Carson with his shoulders.

"Please!"

"It's okay, Mr. Gordeon," Carson interrupted, calming the first sign of panic in his employer's eyes. "Hold the box for me."

Gordeon diverted his attention anxiously between the two men, their eyes locked, excluding him from their undertaking as the box was handed to him. Carson volunteered his arms outward, parallel to his shoulders as Calva moved his hands smoothly, firmly around the man's body.

"And now, Mr. Gordeon, please."

Passing the box back to his companion Gordeon raised his arms above his head, smiling as if quite at ease with the request.

Calva ignored the gesture and the conspiratorial question that followed.

"Is Judd outside the building?"

Calva completed his contact with the soft, tumbling flesh. "Thank you, Mr. Gordeon." Turning, ignoring the question he restarted the downward journey of the elevator.

At the sixth floor the opening doors revealed the Engineer, Tyrell, who stepped inside immediately. Before the elevator began its descent Calva searched the newcomer.

A monotone voice announced their destination, "Ground Floor." Gordeon's metal toe plates tapped the entourage's knotted transition across the marble floor and out of the revolving exit doors. Moving across the boulevard, Calva commanded the pace and direction.

Two walking blocks later, with handkerchief in hand, Gordeon was struggling physically, before Calva slowed to a halt.

"We will wait!" his only instruction as he moved to the curbside.

Gordeon stood behind him and turned to his companions for unspoken approval, for reassurance that the box was still in sight and that he was still safe. Loosening his tie he labored for air.

A taxi moved out of the stream of traffic towards them, its 'Occupe' lights illuminated as Calva raised an arm as if to complete the procedure. He stepped towards the taxi, denying chance access by others as it jerked to a stop next to him.

Claiming the front passenger seat, Calva reached back and swung open the rear passenger door.

Gordeon hesitated at the unspoken invitation.

Calva spoke quietly, out of his open window, directly at Carson.

"Get him into the car or I will leave without you!"

Carson guided the older man forward, prodding his fingertips gently into the middle his back.

"Let's go, Mr. Gordeon!"

Calva faced forward, ignoring the three back seat passengers as the taxi pulled away from the curb and entered the flow of traffic.

Gordeon who, as if to confirm his role, and seated between his entourage, broke the silence of their passage. The hesitancy in his voice betraying his nervousness. His statement issued rhetorically, "This is not my understanding of our arrangement!"

Calva turned his body inward, resting a forearm against the backrest of the seat, his gaze and the muted barrel of his revolver fixed on Gordeon.

"Oh Christ, look, I . . . "

"Please open the package, Mr. Gordeon," the driver interrupted, glancing briefly at the panicked face in his rearview mirror, raising a large, plain envelope to the sight of the passengers.

"Calva, please pass this to Mr. Gordeon. Mr. Gordeon, my name is Ethan Judd. I apologize for the dramatics but you and your consortium partners have made it necessary.."

Gordeon reached for the envelope, resting it on his lap, his eyes downcast, inspecting the gummed seal. Ethan glanced at him through the rearview mirror.

"No, Mr. Gordeon, the micro-film is not there. I have taken the liberty of developing the film, for my own protection, and that of my friends. What you have before you are all twelve pages of the technical summary report in order for you to verify that I in fact do have the complete file. Please open the envelope and verify the contents for yourself."

Gordeon rolled his tongue over his lips and moved the envelope past the view of Calva's gun to Tyrell who nervously forced his fingers into its corner, ripping the crease line of the paper.

"And, Mr. Carson," Ethan continued, "please unwrap your package. Turn the lid towards me and open it. My friend is a very cautious man; he would rather shoot you than risk his life, so I suggest that you open it very slowly and without fault."

Ethan saw the surprise register on the man's face at the use of his name.

"It is not important that you know how, Mr. Carson, but it is important that you are known to me and to others. For future reference, if something were to happen to me. I hope that both you and Mr. Gordeon understand!"

"Look here, Judd, I don't like to be threatened . . . "

"I'm not threatening you, Mr. Gordeon," Ethan interrupted mildly,

pleasantly, raising his eyebrows in mock surprise, "I'm merely stating a
fact of inevitability! If anything happens to me, or to my family, or to my
friends who have assisted me in this endeavor, the same will be exacted
upon you and your children, and your grandchildren. You have used me,
Mr. Gordeon, and it almost cost me my life . . . twice! I will not allow you
a third opportunity without retaliation!"

"Look, Judd, I didn't expect anything like this. I can't control the
Russians or the C . . . "

"The point is irrelevant, Mr. Gordeon. The fact is, my life was
jeopardized and I believe still is! Whether at your specific order," he
continued, catching Carson's glance in the mirror, "or by other interested
parties that you directly or indirectly, knowingly or unknowingly activated!
It is up to you to see that they are called off and that I am left alone. The
success of your efforts will be the continuation of your life and the lives of
your immediate family! There is no further discussion necessary on this
issue. What is left between us is a pure business transaction."

Adjusting the rear-view mirror, Ethan took a long look at Gordeon,
allowing the man to challenge him. There was no need; he knew that he
had won when he heard Carson and Tyrell begin to rip into the wrapping
papers that concealed their divergent treasurers.

He glanced at Tyrell through the mirror, a flush of excitement
showed on the man's face as he studied each of the pages successively
before he gathered and passed them to the rigid Gordeon.

"Sir, they are exactly what I have read before. Mr. Judd must have
the document" was all Tyrell would say, reluctant to look at Gordeon,
unwilling to acknowledge the panic that still registered on his employer's
face following Ethan's warning.

Gordeon folded and slipped the papers into the inner pocket of his suit jacket.

"What about the engineering papers, Mr. Judd? Without them there is nothing. How can we know that you will deliver them?

'Trust, Mr. Gordeon. Trust. Like you, I do not relish looking over my shoulder for the rest of my life. The papers have been deposited with my law firm in Zurich and I know that you have been in communication with them. Once they receive confirmation advice from the bank that you have deposited the funds as agreed, they will release the papers to you."

Picking up speed on the boulevard, Ethan's jugular pounding from the adrenaline rush.

"Gordeon nodded in acknowledgement.

Ethan continued: "Tell me, what was the payment to the Russian émigrés for the delivery of the technology?"

Gordeon paused for affect and looked out of the taxi window as if disdaining interest in the question.

"Permanent US Residence visas and twenty-five million Euros."

Ethan was angry, he wanted to insult the man but he saw the defensive conceit in the face, insulating, masking Gordeon's conscience, defending his ego. Ethan knew that the money was irrelevant to the political and economic power that the holders of the technology could wield.

"How, why did they come to you with the technology? Why not Exxon or Shell or one of the other European players?

"Don't know," Gordeon responded almost gleefully, "all I know is that one day this guy walked into our Zurich with a proposal. A revolutionary power source. If we would open a joint safety deposit box at a bank other than our own, he would deposit a working model of the technology and let it run for three months to prove itself."

"And you said, yes?" Ethan asked.

"Why not! Two keys. One for him and one for us. There was no way for anyone to access the box alone. If it was as good as he said, why not! He told us that it was a nuclear device and that any attempt to break into it would trigger a meltdown. But we were not going to screw with it"

"So what was the outcome?"

Gordeon became quite animated as he recalled the events. 'From what I was told, this guy turns up at the bank with a contraption, about the size of a big soup can, like the ones that you see in restaurants. But this one was solid stainless steel and god knows what else, with an electrical meter and a socket for a light bulb sticking out of the top. It was heavy. The dammdest thing. We took the biggest security room in the bank. He turned the meter on and it starts clicking, he screwed a light bulb into the socket. Both sides locked the room and agreed to meet back there in three months."

All four in the taxi waited for Gordeon to continue.

"Three months later we open the room together and that light bulb was still burning. We figured that the only trick he could have played was to have some known battery technology in the device, but after three months of continuous use, and calculating the energy output from the electrical meter, no way! No way! The rest is history."

Ethan let the story digest before he responded. "You realize that the plan you and Booth conceived was doomed from the outset? Not only did it cost Booth his . . . "

"No, no, no, not at all, Mr. Judd," Gordeon protested defensively. "Yes, Booth's death was unforeseen, but he died while on assignment for the company so his family will be taken care of. The only unforeseen circumstance was the premature transfer of the technology to you! Russian

Internal Security got onto our seller within days of the theft. If the transfer had been accomplished at the Trade Show as planned, we would not be sitting here, in this taxi, wasting my time!"

"So the Iranian meeting was a hoax?" Ethan asked.

"No, it was not Mr. Judd. It was real; it had to be for your alibi to hold.

'But why me, why not have your seller deliver the documents to you electronically or in person somewhere outside of Russia?" Ethan asked.

"We could not risk it. Russia's electronic surveillance would have caught the transfer immediately. On-line encryption is not as safe as we otherwise might believe and our Seller could not draw attention by leaving the country so soon after the technology changed hands; and he certainly was not going to entrust it to anyone; and the longer it stayed in the country the more the risk of discovery by the authorities. Besides, you were a consultant to the Company and if anything went wrong, we could always disown you."

"You mean after the technology was stolen!" Ethan corrected.

"I don't know about the origin of the technology, Mr. Judd. I only know that I am sitting here with you, retrieving, paying a ransom to you for what belongs to us."

Ethan began slowly, quietly, aggressively, "On the contrary My Gordon, you never took possession and you never paid for it. If you have proof-of-ownership, please show it to me." He waited for a response but none followed. "Possession is nine-tenths of the law, Mr. Gordeon, and I have the possession. You and I both know that you blew this one. The biggest deal of your career and you blew it! The only reason that you will succeed is because I am bringing the technology to you. It's costing your shareholders, not that you care, two hundred and fifty million dollars to cover your ego. I know that the amount pales next to the potential value of the technology in the States and so you can justify it to yourself. But remember, Mr. Gordeon, every time somebody congratulates you on your accomplishment, the praise will ring hollow. You will always remember, to your dying day, that it was me who saved your ass and gave you this success."

Turning onto the Rue Madallaine, Ethan headed the taxi back towards the river. "Carson, the box. Open it." Ethan demanded, angry at Gordeon.

Calva sat back, away from the seat, his eyes and his gun riveted to Carson as the man leaned forward and placed the opened mitered cigar box on the top of the seatback.

Gordeon watched both men, his left arm across his chest, countering any imaginary opportunity for the papers to fall from his possession.

Calva reached slowly for the box, placing it on the seat next to him. Carson leaned back, casting his eyes out of the car window, signaling that his part of the transaction was complete.

Calva passed the ornate bundle of bound papers to Ethan who, handling them above the steering wheel, slipped them from their ribbon collar, and scrutinized each individually, as he held the taxi in the line of traffic. Gilt-edged Bank of America Bearer Bonds. Ten of them. Five million US dollars each. He did not like the morality of the bank, but for the moment, their bonds were valued triple AAA and cashing them would not be a problem.

'Thank you, Calva, and now it is your turn." Calva's fingers were his eyes as he randomly extracted the first of a number of objects from the pouch nestled within the box.

Placing his gun next to Ethan's leg, he reached his free hand into his coat pocket and producing a jeweler's glass that he moved to his eye. Tilting his head, catching the light through his fingers, he rolled the stone deftly several times without expression. He placed the stone in his pocket and repeated the process nine more times before he spoke.

"Three carats each, ideal cut. D, flawless, all ten match, they are perfect. Perhaps one hundred and eighty, two hundred thousand dollars each, dealer or auction price!"

Ethan maneuvered the taxi towards the curb, allowing himself a smile.

"Mr. Gordeon, our business if finished. Transfer the cash tomorrow and our dealings are complete." Stopping, double-parked, he turned in his seat. "Before you get out, Mr. Gordeon, answer one question for me. Do you know the symbol of Universal Life?"

Gordeon hesitated. He glanced at Calva and then to Ethan.

"No, I don't. Is it important?"

Ethan smiled, turning forward in his seat he prepared to move back into the stream of traffic as his passengers stepped onto the curb.

"No, it's not important, but you might ask your grandchildren some time soon."

The three men watched the taxi move away into traffic, Gordeon's hand still pressed to the pocket of his coat.

"What the hell did he mean by that, Carson?"

"I have no idea, Mr. Gordeon. I have no idea!"

"Switzerland, Calva. It must be tonight, can you arrange it for me?"

Calva responded with a frown, recognizing the complication that a clandestine entry across the border would present to them if his charge was to remain anonymous as he tucked the diamonds back into their pouch and passed them to Ethan. "I must speak to Staveros!"

Ethan nodded, dropping the pouch into his pocket, his concentration divided between the next step in his plan and the traffic in front of him.

"It must be tonight, Calva. Tonight!"

CHAPTER XXV

135 South. The route decision was Staveros'. The names on the signages: Epernay, Dijon, Lyon were known to Ethan. The distances between them and the count of time were measured in rain and coffee, cigarettes and baguettes; the glare of on-coming traffic balancing the ebb and flow east and west.

Outside of Champagnole, Ethan moved to the bed of the covered truck whose registration and Bills of Lading identified it from Dijon with a load of dry onions, destined for the wholesale market of Genève. Covered with sacking, surrounded by the silent, breathing dome of bagged onions that anchored him, hid him, he gave way to exhaustive sleep before Calva guided the truck into line at the border crossing at La Cure. Two a.m., raining, one of a hundred trucks on schedule to make the markets before sunrise.

The still-quiet roused Ethan's consciousness. Two-thirty by his watch. He stretched slowly in the cramped space, trying to draw the chill and the stiffness from his legs. He realized how comforting the noise and vibration of the truck had been, reinforcing that he was moving, isolated, protected from dangers, at least for a brief time. And now there was silence, speculation of danger, assumptions, until he heard the brothers laughing as they popped the bolts on the cargo doors for inspection.

The Col de la Givrine. They were across the border, heading north, not south towards Genève, north to Lausanne. One more day, one more night.

Preparations to be made. To shave, to wash the odor of onions from his nose and his lungs and from his body; a new shirt, a tie, underwear, socks and shoes; a suit, wool, navy blue, Italian, uniformity with a little flair, and a handkerchief. Three telephone calls: to the Russian Consulate to negotiate for his life; to Renee and Sterne, Genève patent attorneys; and to the United Nations Conference on Environment and Development to conclude his calculated play.

CHAPTER XXVI

Geneva

"Cultural Attaché, please." It was the only way Ethan knew how to make contact. He had nothing to lose.

"Cultural Attaché's office."

"Good morning, my name is Ethan Judd. I would like to speak with the Attaché, please."

"Mm, good morning, sir. May I help you?"

The voice was pleasant. English accent, Russian trained, from the base of the tongue, more flexible in its use than the tip of the tongue that gave the Russians their distinctive pronunciation.

"Yes, good morning. I would like to speak with the Attaché, please."

"For visas, I can help you, sir."

He needed to get past the gate keeper.

"No, thank you. I do not need a visa. I must speak with the Consul. It is most urgent that I speak with the Consul."

"Mm, do you wish to make an appointment, Sir?"

"No. It is most urgent that I speak with the Consul now." He pressed the issue forward. "Is the Consul in his office? This could be a matter of life and death!"

"One moment please."

He waited, expectantly. Success.

"Good morning, my name is Samsonov. May I help you?"

"Yes, good morning. I am holding for the Cultural Attaché."

"I am the Cultural Attaché."

"Mr. Samsonov, thank you for taking my call. My name is Ethan Judd. It is a matter of great urgency that I contact a Mr. Andre Illyach Cosarkov of Russian Internal Security. I do not know where he is located at this time but two days ago he was in Paris." He could sense the hesitancy at the other end of the telephone. "I realize that this is an unusual request and that you do not know me, Mr. Samsonov, but this is a matter of great urgency for me and for the Russian Republic."

"Well, Mr. Judd, this man is not known to me. I do not know where . . ."

"I understand that, Mr. Samsonov," Ethan interrupted, moving over the man's qualifying objection. "I assume that he is known or can be located by others in your Consulate. I repeat, this is a matter of great urgency. I assure you, Mr. Cosarkov will accept my call. I will arrive in Lausanne late this afternoon. Please pass a message to Mr. Cosarkov requesting that he meet with me at the Château d'Ouchy this evening if possible. I will telephone you at six o'clock tonight for confirmation." He paused for emphasis. "Do you understand this message, Mr. Samsonov?"

"Yes, of course, Mr. Judd. I cannot guarantee anything, but I will do my best to pass your message to Mr. Cosarkov."

Ethan broke the connection with a sincere "Thank you."

At precisely 6:05 PM the Cultural Attaché's telephone extension rang once before it was picked up.

"Mr. Judd?"

Ethan recognized the voice.

"Mr. Cosarkov! It is good to hear your voice. How is your leg?"

He did not wait for a reply. "Are you here in Lausanne or is this call being relayed to you?"

"No, I am here in Lausanne, Mr. Judd. I flew in this afternoon, from Paris. This was your request, was it not? And my leg will heal, thank you for asking."

There were no other pleasantries. They understood each other.

"Yes, that was my request. Thank you for your effort." Ethan slowed the conversation. "I would like to meet with you, Mr. Cosarkov. Alone, tonight, if possible! You will understand that I did not bring my luggage with me and that I have taken certain precautions for its retrieval should anything unforeseen happen to me. I am willing to negotiate with you. But only you, and alone."

Cosarkov's voice was passive.

"Yes, of course, Mr. Judd. The time and place are yours."

"Meet me outside the Château d'Ouchy at eight-thirty. If I am not there on time please wait at least fifteen minutes."

Cosarkov repeated the time and place.

"Should I bring anything with me, Mr. Judd?"

"No, nothing is required."

The reflective windows of the restaurant provided Ethan a clear view of the hotel's facade across the promenade. He watched Cosarkov approach the entrance. He watched the man turn, towards the curb, leaning heavily on a pair of crutches. He had watched everyone who had entered the restaurant in the last hour and now he watched the traffic, the pedestrians, Cosarkov, for what he hoped would not be there. He needed to trust the Russian. He needed an ally. He watched Cosarkov as he turned and leaned against the building, resting the crutches beside him, waiting.

Ethan's telephone call to the Doorman of the hotel was short. He watched the man approach the recipient of his message. He watched Cosarkov slip onto his crutches and begin a rhythmical loop towards the restaurant. Ethan could see none that followed. He needed to trust the man. Calva sat, seeing but unseen on the promenade wall. It was a comfort, but he needed to trust Cosarkov.

Ethan stood and extended his hand as Cosarkov approached the table.

"Well, Mr. Judd." Cosarkov smiled, laying the crutches on the chair between them. "I am alone and, as you can see, not able to do much of anything else except to listen."

The two men studied each other before Ethan spoke.

"My first name is Ethan, may I call you Illyach?"

Cosarkov raised an eyebrow, feigning surprise.

"I see that the Israelis have filled you in already, Ethan! I would be pleased if you would call me Illyach, but, whether we are to be friends' remains to be seen!"

Ethan nodded.

"Actually, it was the Americans who told me who you were."

Cosarkov's surprise was real.

"The Americans! We . . . I did not think that you had gone that far. We had no idea that you were working for . . ."

"Actually, Illyach, believe it or not, I'm not working for the Americans. I'm not working for the Israelis, nor for your émigré group. Yes, I was the courier of the micro-film, but I had no idea as to what was going on until the Israelis told me in Paris three days ago, and even that was not on a voluntary basis!"

"So, that explains why you are still on the run."

They fell silent, as espresso was presented. Ethan was the first to speak.

"You are a Major in the Regular Army, Illyach?"

"Was. Infantry. Three tours in Afghanistan."

"Wounded?"

"Twice, and one case of gonorrhea, I was not married at the time. And you?"

Ethan smiled for the first time that he could remember as he volunteered what was never spoken of. Perhaps it was the neutrality of his confessor, but it came easily.

"Vietnam. Captain, U.S. Rangers. Two tours. Wounded twice."

Cosarkov raised his cup. "To ghosts."

"To ghosts." Ethan smiled, reciprocating the gesture, sipping the draft slowly.

"It's actually because we were both soldiers, Illyach that I asked for you, that I asked for you to be here. I now know what I have. I have some idea of the value of the technology. I want to make a deal to get myself out of this, this situation."

Cosarkov was passive as he lit a cigarette and offered the pack across the table. He waited for Ethan to continue.

"I have filed patents on the technology here in Switzerland."

"You have what?" Cosarkov questioned with surprise.

"Yes, and I have assigned certain of those rights. Firstly, to the Americans, to the company that arranged for the transfer, the theft or whatever you want to call it. They used me to courier the documents. I have not transferred any rights to the U.S. government. The government was never part of the play, as far as I know."

"What was your deal?"

"Two hundred and fifty million U.S. dollars, one million dollars in diamonds, and a pledge of no retaliation!"

"So little, my friend!" Cosarkov exclaimed skeptically. "If you know the value of the technology, why not five hundred million or even one billion? That is a small amount in today's world, even in Russia?"

"More than enough!" Ethan smiled, "I am a man of simple tastes and besides, I don't have to defend it, it is done. I have also assigned certain rights to the Israelis."

"For helping you?"

Ethan shrugged.

"For helping me, and for neutralizing the émigrés. I plan to give them twenty-five million dollars, their original selling price, to back off.

Cosarkov pressed no further.

"And so you have two hundred and twenty-five million!"

"There are other expenses to cover as well. And I'm giving a technology license to the French." Ethan answered the question before it came. "I enjoy Paris and I don't want problems in the future. Who knows, I might want to settle there."

"The cost?"

"Neutrality, no claims what-so-ever. I want your government to re-enforce this with the French for me."

Cosarkov nodded silently again.

"You are walking a fine line, my friend, considering that the technology was stolen from us in the first place!"

"A very fine line," Ethan smiled, "but once the technology becomes public, you will never be able to claim its return. And that, Illyach, is why I want to discuss the last two issues with you. I want to make the same assignment to your government as I gave the French and the Israelis. An exclusive, irrevocable, royalty free license, but this time covering all of the old Soviet Republics, no retaliation against me and no further claims on the technology. This is what I ask. You came too close in the aquifers Illyach not to demand it openly and clearly."

"Ah, therein may lie a problem for us! Cosarkov gestured, tapping an ashtray idly with his cigarette.

"Meaning?"

"Meaning that it was not us in the aquifers who were shooting at you! Nor was it the French! That much I know for sure. My assignment was, and continues to be, the retrieval of our State secrets. Thanks to you, thanks to your call, what I thought was failure has, possibly, been resurrected, at least for the time-being. My direct assignment never was to eliminate you, at least not until all other avenues of retrieving the technology had failed. More about covering a messy problem rather than taking revenge upon you."

Ethan was silent, shocked by the revelation of another party involved.

"Then who? The Americans? The government or commercial interests?"

"We don't know for sure, we don't think so. We have communicated through our own channels within your government and we don't think so," Cosarkov replied, "perhaps Vory V'zakone."

"I understand the translation, Thieves in Law, but I don't know this name." Ethan responded.

"No, you probably would not. Their existence in the West is relatively new. Without giving you a lesson in Russian history, they are what you would call a secret criminal society. They go back to the time of the Czars. In those days they were more elitist, more refined. Today its membership has been expanded to include government officials at the highest levels of power, ex-KGB and military at the highest echelon.. They are the elite of the Russian Mafia."

"But why would they come after me?" Ethan did not wait for an answer. "Did your people burgle my hotel rooms in Moscow and Prague? And who killed Booth in Paris?

Cosarkov smiled matter-of-factly.

"Not us in Moscow, not us in Prague and not us in Paris. We were always one step behind you. Our only luck was in locating your advance room booking in Paris. There, we arrived and just waited, but we could not understand how you stayed ahead of us without help from within our own ranks. Always one step ahead. There was the highest priority, the highest secrecy placed on this affair. We believed that you might have been part of the Vory V'zakone, with knowledge from within. Always one step ahead.

Ethan shook his head with finality.

"No, Absolutely not. I am a man way out of my depth on this one, Illyach!"

"Well, no matter for the moment. Your safety may depend on what you and I decide upon here, tonight."

Ethan looked at Cosarkov intently.

"No, no my friend, not from me, not from us. At least not until after I hear your proposition in full and decide." Cosarkov responded as he lifted his coffee demitasse and watched for Ethan's reaction. "You said you wanted to discuss two issues with me!"

"Tell me why these people would come after me if they knew that Russian Internal Security was involved?" Ethan queried, deferring the beginning of the next part of their conversation.

"Opportunity, confidence," Cosarkov shrugged, "exploitation of the moment. We don't think that they knew about the technology until after it was stolen. Then, the race was on. You were, you are the rabbit with the carrot."

Ethan listened without distraction as Cosarkov continued: "With few restrictions on travel today, and with satellite phones and computers, the world is the market place for these people. Anywhere the old Jewish Mafia emigrated to in the 70's and 80's, this new group has taken over." Laughing, he continued, "some of them even claimed Jewish ancestry to help hasten their exit visas. Your American 'Sixty Minutes' television show reported a little on them a couple of years ago when smuggled Russian nuclear materials ended up in Germany on its way to the Middle East. But you and I are talking about history. The old style Vory V'zakone, the Tsarist Vory V'zakone was a world of money laundering, of government contracts and diamond smuggling, of small time extortion. But it also had its fingers into the heart of the Soviet Central Politburo since Lenin's time. That is why Stalin killed so many Jews. He feared their secret society, their support of his political opposition. Did you know this, my friend?"

Ethan let him continue without reply.

"That the Western countries did not intervene in any way is because the Vory V'zakone survived. It still has its political value today, to both sides. But believe me, it is nothing like the old guard. The new bosses have changed the rules of the engagement. They changed the nature of crime in Russia and now the world. In a slightly different way, they mirror the control, the, the moral corruption of the top echelon of the global capitalist companies, but they are not as blatant in their activities. "
Ethan digested his predicament in the silence that followed.

"Do you have firsthand knowledge of this new Russian Mafia, Illyach?"

"I do, my friend, some of the highest profile companies in Russia today are under their control and," Cosarkov followed, smiling, pointing a finger to his chest and then at Ethan, "if I did not follow the instinct that I have here, I would think that you are one of them!"

Ethan cocked his head in lieu of a response as Cosarkov continued:

"Stolen Russian nuclear technology, your ability to stay out of our reach and that of the American and French governments, and your payments: negotiable U.S. Bank Bonds and diamonds, and an uncanny network of support in Paris that got you out of the aquifers, away from the Israelis, away from all of us. Now," he emphasized, leaning back in his chair, "you surface in Switzerland, in your own time, with your own agenda and demands! What else should I think?"

Ethan smiled as he lit another cigarette and inhaled gently.

"Thank you for your trust, Illyach."

"I hope that it is founded in truth otherwise, I don't know what use I could be to you. Unless you want to turn yourself in to me!"

Ethan chattered his head from side to side quickly.

"It's not in my plans, Illyach."

"Then tell me what is, my friend?"

Ethan paused and watched the air bubbles that rose to the surface of the sugar cubes that he dipped and released into the surface of the espresso before he began again.

"I had assumed that it was either you or the émigré group in Moscow and Prague and Paris, Illyach, and that I would be able to negotiate a return of the technology in return for safe passage, a way out. But now, it seems that there is another element to deal with. One that you acknowledge you have no control over."

"You are correct on this point, Ethan, but tell me, what is your plan? Perhaps it will work for both of us!"

"My intent is to assign an exclusive license of the technology to the Republic of Russia, to France and to Israel, and," he broke into a smile, "what if I assign a non-exclusive worldwide license to the United Nations for use in any other country that requests it? This would negate any interest by anyone else to having access or control of the technology. It would come at a cost, of course!"

"You want to create a new world order, Ethan. From such humble beginnings to a global policy maker."
"No, not really Illyach, but can you think of any other way to lay this thing to rest? Cosarkov was quiet, digesting, calculating the ramifications.

"You have balls, my friend. I will say that for you. But why would you do this?"

"Your people, and the French and the Israelis, will get the technology at no cost. The American government can negotiate with the company that started the whole mess and I figure, if the technology is public, there is no reason to come after me."

"That would certainly take the Vory V'zakone out of the picture for you." Cosarkov agreed with the logic.
Ethan waited.

"What is the cost that you want from the U.N.?"

"Well, I'm thinking laterally here, so bare with me." Ethan began, studying the demi-cup as if for inspiration, "I'm a little angry, Illyach, perhaps frustrated is a better word. I'm a citizen of the southern hemisphere. I remember being told once that over sixty percent of our population during the next twenty years will develop some form of skin cancer, cataracts or problems with their immune system. All attributable to solar ultraviolet radiation and the depleting ozone layer. I'm not fanatical about it, but when you are outside, you can feel an intensity of the sun that I did not remember as a boy; and today, maybe I am in a position to do something about it! This is my atmosphere, my children's support system. They, and perhaps one day my grandchildren could be one of those statistics and this is unacceptable to me, especially for the economic gain of a handful of multi-national companies a hemisphere away, with government complicity. The United States, Western Europe, Japan, China, even Russia. To be dramatic, it would be a self-fulfilling prophecy if the human race's giant meteor was called ozone, and then we went the way of the dinosaurs." Cosarkov let him continue uninterrupted: "I remember in a book that Al Gore wrote in the late eighties, early nineties, a statement that he made on the last page, something to the effect that it would be sad if the next generation could not look up to the sky because of the fear of solar ultraviolet radiation, all tied into ozone depletion! That comment has always stayed with me."

Ethan sipped his coffee before he continued.

"I am a father of two . . ." he corrected himself, "three children, Illyach. Children of the next generation, as are your two, one yet unborn. I am a man not outside of the mainstream of normal thinking or behavior, and today maybe I, can contribute something to the survival of our planet. I can contribute something to our world. Perhaps only for one day. Perhaps only for today! I did not create it, but I have it in my possession and I'm going to exploit it, with your help!"

"So, you are going to save the world! Such a burden you carry for all of us, my friend."

Ethan looked up sharply.

"Actually, it's not, Illyach. Cynically I suppose, I have always thought that the northern hemisphere countries would do something about the ozone issue when a winter hole developed over the Arctic, over their own heads. Well, it happened in the mid-nineties. From the Arctic to Florida in winter and over most of Northern Europe, including Russia but there is no hue or cry. This aside, what do you suggest that I do with the technology? What sort of statement do you think that I should make with it?"

Cosarkov was exacerbated.

"I don't know, Ethan, but I don't see you as a spokesman for the developing countries, telling the industrialized world to bugger-off and then taking your two hundred million dollars and just disappearing. And after the Japanese earthquake and their nuclear plant problems, I am not at sure that anyone will have much of an appetite to step up the plate for quite some time"

'You may be right, Illyach, but sooner or later it will happen. Probably about the time of six dollar a gallon gas and a statement from the nuclear power industry that this new technology does not require the obsolete technology of the past and that they have learned by the Japanese mistakes and that the manufacturing facilities will be absolutely failsafe. It will be a bit like BP in the Gulf and Chevron and Shell Oil in Nigeria." Ethan continued matter-of-factly, "Illyach, I'm not naive enough to think that the industrialized powers will not try to negate all of this away, especially any rights to the developing countries, but it is a simple beginning, and I can do it, so why not! Perhaps it will trigger something positive elsewhere in the world. Hell, maybe the developing countries will get access to the technology if they stop stripping the Amazon for grazing land and Indonesia for timber. Maybe if they stop burning coal as a god given right in order to catch up with the west. I don't know, but there are people out there doing good things, you know? And who knows, maybe I can leave the world a little better than it was when I came into it. I had thought about planting a forest, but."

Cosarkov leaned back in his chair and smiled at Ethan's irreverent shrug.

"Well, Mr. Johnny Appleseed, I don't think that you are naïve and yes I will help you . . . on three conditions."

"Name them."

"One, my orders were to retrieve the technology. So I must return to Moscow with it in my possession."

"Not a problem. You will have your copy tomorrow."

"Two," Cosarkov nodded, counting on his fingers, "this technology was actually stolen by us from the United States, so may I suggest, for good order, that you do assign the license rights to the United Nations in the name of The Republic of Russia and The United States, in that order, unless your ego is such that you want your name on it!" Ethan smiled.

"Consider it done."

"Good, then I believe that this will neutralize any ill-will at home. I will tell them that I got to you too late, which is true! Fait accompli, as though to speak. It will be my reasoning, my justification and, more importantly for you, as I said before, taking the technology public to the world should negate any reason for the Vory V'zakone to follow you. Their opportunity will have disappeared."

Ethan nodded, acknowledging the logic.

"And your third condition?"

"That you give me the name of the U.S. licensee before it becomes public knowledge. I have no experience with the New York Stock Exchange, but I think that this might be a good time to try it. At least once, don't you think?" he smiled.

Ethan leaned forward, over the table, his voice quiet.

"Illyach, I will have two hundred million dollars from this transaction. What can I offer you?"

Cosarkov rested his jaw on the palm of his hand. He cocked his head and frowned.

"An important question, my friend. Nothing for the moment, I have an assignment for my country to finish, but we can talk when all of this is finished. Another time, another place. Speaking of which, my leg is sore, my body is tired, and I must sleep."

Ethan reached across the table and offered his hand as they both stood.

"Done! The time and place are yours. We will keep in touch."

"Oh, one thing, Ethan! Your communiqué was passed to me in Paris this afternoon. I may not have been the only one to read it, nor to have an airplane at my immediate disposal. So, may I suggest that you spend the night in the safety of the Consulate with me!"

Ethan felt his adrenaline rush. Too early to trust that far, too early.

"Thank you, Illyach, it is a kind offer, but as you can understand, I feel the need to move on my own. But we shall talk early tomorrow morning. There are arrangements that I will ask you to make."

Cosarkov acknowledged the statement as he collected the crutches, "Until tomorrow then."

"Right, until tomorrow, Illyach."

CHAPTER XXVII

The steps, twenty-three, white, granite, serrated under the soles of his leather shoes, leading to the UNESCO building seemed like a coronation row. On any other occasion he would have enjoyed the drive into Genève, entering the city from the north, skirting the lake, riding in the cab of the truck, high above the streets, across the Pont du Mont Blanc where the waters of the Rhone redefined themselves with the Lac Leman, but not today. Today the tightness in his chest reminded him that he was about to commence a journey that would change his life, irretrievably, forever. No approvals, just his own decision, his own commitment. He was nervous, aware of that insecure part of his psyche that screamed to re-examine, to abort the decisions that he had made, to rationalize another compromise beyond those he had already negotiated.

He sat quietly as Calva maneuvered the truck to a dead stop at the curbside. Immobile, he waited for an inner trigger to activate his exit from the vehicle.

Calva held the truck in gear, his foot riding the clutch, watching the approaching traffic through the rearview mirror. His concentration did not waiver as Ethan exhaled deeply and leaned into the door, opening it, stepping onto the curb.

He allowed himself a long, deliberate panorama of the square before he addressed Calva through the open window.

"Please deliver this to Staveros."

Calva leaned across the seat, the palm of his hand outstretched to receive the package that Ethan produced from his jacket pocket.

"Tell him that it is a gesture that does not equal the value of his friendship nor the honor of his family." He hesitated, looking for the words, conscious of the emotion that he felt. He remembered a similar moment, unspoken, far away, when he left his platoon in Nam, boarding a chopper out of the fire zone for the last time. He hadn't abandoned them, but he remembered his utter, utter feeling of lonely emptiness. He felt a similar kinship with the man sitting in front of him now in the truck. Kinship of life and the possibility of death shared together, no matter the duration. But this time, he did not want his feelings to go unspoken. He did not want to carry it, a regret of unwillingness, of hesitancy to express what he felt for the rest of his time as he carried his regret from Nam. He needed to say good-bye.

Calva recognized his difficulty but said nothing.

"Tell Staveros, tell him that his family is now my family. Someday my debt to all of you shall be repaid."

Calva nodded solemnly, absorbing his words, through the eyes, for his brother.

"And, Calva, your bravery and that of Rabio, and your loyalty, do you much honor."

He pressed the paper package into Calva's open hand, a soldier's smile upon his cheeks. He squeezed the man's wrist. His words were finished. He felt his loneliness, but this time he rejoiced, knowing that he could feel it, knowing that he could celebrate that feeling in his heart.

Calva did not take his eyes from the back of the strange American until the man began his ascent from the square to the steps of the building and was absorbed in the flow of pedestrian traffic. He did not open the double folded gilt-edged sheets of bond paper emblazed with an American eagle. There was no need. And he had felt the knobby lump folded within them. He knew what it was. Placing the makeshift envelope into his coat pocket, he leaned out of the truck window and, signaling with a wave of his hand, moved into the boulevard traffic.

CHAPTER XXVIII

Ethan began his words hesitantly. He had never been sure how to address a solitary woman in an audience. Ignoring the empty chairs, he concentrated his attention on the three journalists seated in front of him; recognizing that their presence was dictated only by their assignment to the United Nations Conference on Environment and Development and the request of the Russian and French embassies. He did not introduce the men, seated behind him, strangers to him less than twenty-four hours ago.

"Good morning, ladies and gentlemen. All three of you are here because of your assignments to UNESCO . . . not because of me."

He watched the journalists turn their attention to him, the openness of his honesty piquing their interest.

"Today, I am turning over to the United Nations Conference on Environment and Development, on behalf of the governments of The Republic of Russia and The United States of America, the licensing rights to a revolutionary energy technology, the international patent applications for which were filed this morning on behalf of the indigenous peoples of the world and assigned to the United Nations.

"First conceived in the United States, this technology was refined and commercialized with contributions from the American and Russian governments. Like the space program, it is another gesture towards world peace and the protection of our environment. The technology is not from the realm of known nuclear physics. No fission, no fusion, only a resonant electric circuit contained within a storage vessel the size of a ten-liter drum, capable of utilizing today's nuclear waste, capable of generating enough electricity to power the average European household for twenty to thirty years.

"UNCED will act as trustee of the dissemination of this technology to the world community, in accordance with the instructions of the indigenous spokesmen and women of those developing countries who either sit on the Counsel or who will soon join it, having fought their battles for environmental sanity and preservation from behind the corruption of national politics. What has traditionally been one of the weakest and most ineffective of all the United Nations' agencies it is hoped will now become one of its most powerful." He paused, realizing that even his opinion was being recorded as fact.

"They will negotiate the licensing of this technology on a country by country basis. The price, a one year phase-out and the permanent halt in the production and utilization of ozone depleting gases worldwide, the halt of all destruction of forests and jungle clearing and the conversion of all power generation from fossil fuels to the utilization of this new technology.

"Licensing arrangements have been concluded separately in the United States and with the Russian Republic and the Israeli government and," he hesitated, turning and gesturing to the three men seated behind him, "negotiations are underway with France. Representatives from those governments are present here today. UNCED will negotiate for the return of native lands and resources, for the future of our children's children. For what we know but do not put into action, the simple, sustainable survival of our planet."

Looking back again at the men behind him, Ethan gestured with a raise of his head.

"I would draw special attention to Mr. Andre Illyach Cosarkov of the Russian Republic who is seated to my left. He, too, is a family man with," he remembered the man's words, 'one daughter and one yet unborn.' Andre has worked very closely with me to secure the future of this technology for his country and for the world. Without him I might not be here today, none of this might have happened!"

He watched the Russian smile, a private joke of the reality between them.

"Despite the handicap of a painful accident wound, Andre has been instrumental in working with and coordinating the efforts of both the Russian and the French governments and the American and Israeli licensees." To the journalists he admonished, "and please be sure to spell his name correctly ..."

Smiling again towards the Russian, he continued, his debt paid, his negotiations competed. Illyach would be a household name in Russia, at least in those circles that mattered, his future, like that of Gorbachov, assured.

"The United Nations Conference on Environment and Development now has a common denominator for the sustainable use of the earth's resources that should be acceptable to both the North and the South. There is hope that all of the nations of our planet should embrace this goodwill in a spirit of common survival."

The silence that followed, the sound of his footsteps as he left the podium confirmed that the enormity of the political consequences of the announcement was not lost on his audience; the pandemonium of questions that erupted, directed towards Cosarkov, the bewildered Frenchman whom he had never met, and the unprepared U.N. representative, reinforced his cynicism that he had become a past player already.

CHAPTER XXIX

"You are a very unusual man, Mr. Judd. May I be the first to congratulate you!"

Ethan registered the voice as he turned towards the woman standing inside the curtained wings of the stage. She had positioned herself deliberately to intercept him as he exited the podium, two others discretely out of earshot.

"How did you know.. I was hoping that you would be here," he finished with a smile, stopping to take both of her hands as she offered them. "Did you hear all of it?"

Madame Simone raised her eyebrows, "A little dramatic perhaps, but I believe that I understood your motives. I might say that you were very generous to the Russian, Cosarkov. You have secured a bright future for him within the Russian power brokers. He owes you a great deal."

"Perhaps," he shrugged, a deferring acknowledgment of her observations.

"And do you approve of my decisions?"

"It is not a matter of approval, Mr. Judd, the actions were yours alone. But, as I said, you are a very unusual man." She continued as he released her hands.

"A man of conscience, a man who follows his heart."

Ethan dropped his eyes to a point somewhere between and behind her skirt and the wooden floor, embarrassed at the statement that she volunteered with the sparkle in her eyes.

"Well, at least this time!" he exclaimed, reaching into his suit jacket pocket, producing two sealed envelopes and passing one of them openly to her.

"This one is for your government and the other is for your Russian émigrés. For them, thirty million US dollars in bearer bonds, it is roughly the amount in Euros that they negotiated in the first place for their sale of the technology to the Americans. And for Israel, an irrevocable license for the technology itself. I would hope that this will settle matters between us."

"Thank you, Mr. Judd," she said, weighing the envelopes in her hands. "I will see that both parties understand your need for privacy. I'm sure that they will wish you long life." Smiling, she continued, "And the envelope for me, tell me, do you do this for Israel, or for Laxmi, or for yourself?"

Ethan absorbed the expanse of the backstage area without visualizing it. He smiled openly, feeling the lightness that he was beginning to feel.

"Let's just say that I did it for all of the thoughts that I am at this moment, today!"

Smiling, Madame Simone recognized that this was all of the answer that she was going to get.

"And what of the Americans, Ethan? Their exclusive agreement with you, it has turned out to be not so exclusive?"

"They transferred their money this morning. And my agreement, it was a verbal negotiation. I never referred or inferred worldwide exclusivity, and besides, the exclusivity of the United States market should be enough for any company. I have probably saved them from all sorts of international political and economic intrigue if it had been otherwise!"

"Did you plan it this way?"

"No," he smiled, shaking his head, "it just happened. But I don't think that they want the Russian government to know of their duplicity with the Iranians, especially as they have on-going business together and they can deal with the United States government in whatever manner they want."

The woman nodded in acknowledgment.

"I think that the Russians know about the Iranian deal, but that's another story.'

This letter is for you, Ethan," she continued," I hope that its contents match those of your heart."

She reached with the palm of her hand to his cheek and smiled softly.

"Twenty-five years ago, I might also have written to you," Moving her head back and forth in a gesture of resignation she dropped her hands to her sides and smiled, "but now . . . Good-bye and long-life, Mr. Ethan Judd, oh, and Happy Pesach."

"Good-bye" he whispered, turning, moving, alone, towards the stage door exit of the building, as unknown as he was when he had entered it. Dark glasses shaded his eyes, allowing him the freedom to see without being seen as he left the building and moved towards the boulevard. He half-hoped to see Calva waiting for him at the square. But he did not look. He knew that his soldier was long gone.

Nor did he look back at the building, at the square, as the taxi, gathering momentum, accelerated him towards the airport. He watched the muted colors of the buildings and the shop windows as they passed his window. He held the envelope gently to his lips, breathing a memory, aware of his driver who sat in a different world.

With a deep breath of finality, he opened the envelope, careful not to tear the paper content that he would carry into his future. He began to read:

My Dearest Ethan. What emotion I am going through with you, so much intensity of feelings. I know the passion between us is like a magnet, the attraction, and I long for more. Already I miss being with you, touching you is so healing. My heart fills with the excitement of being with you, things to share and discover, together.

Ours was not the easiest of beginnings for a relationship but things unfold in their own time, in their own way. Now, my love, that you are in my heart, for always, I will not break that bond.

I see you breaking from a long and binding past and wanting to begin anew with fulfillment of your own needs and trying hard to achieve it, but the transition is still in process and the 'break' is still fresh. You can see what you want, but don't want to hurt anyone in the process, and because there is still pulling on both sides, it goes back and forth with you. I guess you are making that decision to choose, to follow your heart. Time is the factor, at least that's what I see, because a person cannot move by playing both sides of the fence, or sitting in the middle like you. I have never been in this situation.

I write about these things because of how I feel. Sometimes it's risky being open, especially since our time together has been so short — but it is said from my heart.

I long to explore a relationship with you. You asked me if my activities in Paris were natural for me, and I did not answer you. They were, but not with you, and no longer. I have resigned and am returning to Tel Aviv this afternoon. I may have appeared as strong, a survivor, but I too long for more. Love, friendship, devotion, support through the trials that life brings.

Sometimes, deep down, all I want to do is to relax in a partner's arms and to be the little child I am. I say sometimes because it is a balance of being the comforted and the comforter. If I were truly strong, I would depend more on the true comforter who can cradle me — of this I know to be the truth. Maybe you are a hard lesson for me, for I am still longing for a constant and loving companion as well.

I do not wish to crowd your space, for I, too, am a creature of balance but I want my partner close. Otherwise, it tips my scales out of balance and then I have to work too hard on the inside. The balance is within, and without, and then I am happy.

Our lives have touched. You are in my heart. I feel like rolling over and over and over with you, wrapped in your arms and telling you that I love you. Je t'aime. Laxmi.

CHAPTER XXX

In the El Al lounge Ethan was alone in his thoughts, acknowledging the decision he was about to make for himself. The imprinted subconscious of his childhood experiences called subtly for him to ignore the feelings that were his heart. He was off-balance and he was tired. He knew it. His mind, enabled for so many years for the good of others, dutiful father, faithful husband before his divorce, called him back to a space of comfortable non-commitment, to a place of neutrality that he had occupied for so many empty years. Now, he was about to commit to an unknown future. Flashes of guilt assailed his thoughts, pressing him to reconsider his decision: his children, halfway around the world, growing up without him; he would visit, but was it enough, for him, for them? And Samera, Mitriann's Samera; how to begin.

He could not answer his hesitancy. For the first time in so many years, he would have to listen and trust in himself. A different kind of trust, a different kind of listening. So much easier to return to the States, perhaps to try and put the marriage back together. He wanted to be physically close to his children, to grow with them. But deep in his heart he knew that the reason he had left his marriage was the same reason he could not return to it. It was not the children. Sooner or later he would feel the same needs again, the same longings of expression that Laxmi had opened within him. Any compromise now would not be fair to himself, nor to his children, nor to his ex-wife. "God, what to do!" The decision was his. For the first time in so very long, he shut his eyes, hard, forcing the brightest of light to appear in his consciousness, and he prayed.

He sat through two flight announcements, his heart pounding for himself, for his future, unknown, hesitant; until, as the final announcement was made, with boarding pass held lightly between his fingers, he moved towards the blinking El Al gate 'Flight 348 TEL AVIV IMMEDIATE BOARDING'.

ABOUT THE AUTHOR

RS is the author of several screen plays including The Communion of Dan Webo and The Making of an MP. Manuscripts in progress include: The Rag Trade and Shall We Dance? Raised in New Zealand he has spent most of his international working career in the US and the UK. He now lives in Seattle with his family.

He scribes when the voices come.

www.ingramcontent.com/pod-product-compliance
Lightning Source LLC
Chambersburg PA
CBHW060056150626
46556CB00017BA/1110